SENTINALS RECOVERY

D1549385

SENTINALS RECOVERY

HELEN GARRAWAY

Published by Jerven Publishing

Cover by Jeff Brown Graphics

Map by Fictive Designs

This is a work of fiction. Names, characters, organisations, places, events, and incidents are either products of the author's imagination or are used fictitiously. Any resemblance to actual events or persons, living or dead, businesses, companies or locales is entirely coincidental.

eBook ISBN: 978-1-7399344-0-8

Paperback ISBN: 978-1-7399344-1-5

Hardback ISBN: 978-1-7399344-2-2

Sign up to my mailing list to join my magical world and for further information about forthcoming books and latest news at: www.helengarraway.com

First Edition

For my cousin, Maria

*Hoping this tempts you
into the world of Remargaren*

CONTENTS

1

Birlerion woke in a panic. Gasping for air, he struggled out of the constraining blankets. He couldn't breathe. His mouth was full of dirt, clogging his throat, suffocating him. Tears trailed down his cheeks as he dragged in a desperate gulp of air, chest aching at the effort.

Warm arms embraced him. "Hush, you're safe, Birlerion. Concentrate on your breaths, one at a time."

Birlerion writhed, inhaling more noise than air. His face darkened as his lungs failed to take in enough, and he shuddered as the stench of burning flesh filled his nose. He clutched the material beneath his fingers, and the arms around him tightened.

"You're safe in your sentinal. You can control it. That's right. One breath, two breaths …"

Birlerion collapsed, exhausted, his throat raw, his chest heavy. He inhaled, chest heaving, and exhaled a wheezing sigh, concentrating on the effort. He relaxed as the soft touch of his sentinal embraced him, and then darkness claimed him.

Much later, soft voices woke him, and he lay concentrating on the simple mechanics of getting air into his lungs. In and out. Why was it so difficult to breathe? His chest was tight, uncomfortable. Voices percolated into his awareness, and his brow wrinkled as he tried to place them.

"He needs more time. We can't move him yet. He's not stable enough."

"The grand duke has recalled all his men; the plateau is deserted. It's been nearly two months since the battle, Marguerite. How much longer will it take?"

"As long as it needs to. He nearly died, Taurillion. His chest was crushed. It takes time to rebuild, to heal."

"Then how did he survive?"

The light changed above Birlerion as a soft hand smoothed his forehead. Marguerite sighed, her breath a warm caress on his cheek. "Birlerion?" She leaned over him, and he opened his eyes. As her precious face hovered above him, her vivid blue eyes were full of concern, though she was quick to hide it. She smiled at him.

"Hi," she said.

Birlerion stared at her, an impossibility. She had bonded with the land, hadn't she? "Marguerite?" he croaked, raising a shaky hand. By the Lady, he felt weak. He rested his hand on her arm, rubbing the auburn curls between his trembling fingers. She was real. "How are you here? Did we win?"

"Of course we won. You did it. You shielded the Captain long enough for him to strike."

Birlerion flinched against the flood of memories: the terrible winds, Leyandrii and Guerlaire falling as the ground ripped apart, being consumed by the Land … "Leyandrii fell. Is she alright?"

"She's fine."

"And the Captain?"

"He had to leave. He is in Old Vespers with the king."

Birlerion dropped his hand, exhausted by the effort. He

cleared his throat; the taste of rain and fresh soil filled his mouth. "King? What king? Where are Leyandrii and Guerlaire?"

Marguerite hesitated and exchanged glances with Taurillion. She reached for a glass. "They are fine. Here, drink. You must be thirsty. Just take small sips."

Taurillion helped Birlerion sit up, and he sipped the water while resting against Taurillion's solid chest, catching his breath in between. If he took the gulps he wanted, he thought he might drown. He lay back on his pillow, breathless, his chest wheezing.

"What happened to me?"

"You got in the way of an Ascendant, and he blasted you in the chest," Taurillion replied.

Birlerion stared at the copper-eyed Sentinal as the memories filtered in. "It was Clary, wasn't it? He just won't stop hounding me."

"I think that's enough talking for now," said Marguerite. "Rest, Birlerion. We'll talk more later."

Obediently closing his eyes, Birlerion relaxed into the soft embrace of his sentinal. The hum deepened in concern, and Birlerion hurried to reassure him that he was fine. Then his awareness melted away, and he slept.

Marguerite looked down at him. His black hair had grown and now curled around his neck, accentuating the translucence of his skin. His face, relaxed in sleep, was all hollow angles and curves, with dark lashes hiding mesmerising silver eyes. Once, they had been an equally mesmerising indigo. His cheeks were sunken and he had lost weight, a result of the huge discharge of magic he had made; too much.

On top of that, he had taken the full brunt of an Ascendant lord's anger. It was amazing that he lived. She wasn't sure how it was possible. The healer had proclaimed him dead, but Ari, the little Arifel, and his sentinal had refused to believe it.

As his chest rose, she knew that, although the horrific burns had been healed by his sentinal, his lungs were struggling to fill the space that his newly rebuilt rib cage provided. If that was not enough, he was also confused. Unsurprising, she supposed. She should have anticipated it.

The next morning, Birlerion lay for a moment, adjusting. Something was off but he wasn't sure what. As he pondered, Ari, the small brown and black coloured kitten-like creature with scaly wings and tail popped into view and landed on his chest. Ari crooned as he flipped his wings back and walked up Birlerion's chest to rub his head against Birlerion's face. For such a small creature, his feet felt like bricks, bruising his skin, and Birlerion shuffled upright as he picked the little Arifel up and cuddled him.

"Ari, what are you doing here?" he thought as the creature bombarded him with images. *"Slow down, I can't make sense of it all."*

The images slowed and Birlerion saw himself and Jerrol on the plateau above the plains of Oprimere, and he remembered everything that had happened. Well, up to a certain point. Ari crooned again, snuggling up against his neck. He wrapped his tail around Birlerion's throat, and a soft vibration shivered through Birlerion.

Birlerion leaned back against his cushions, soothed. *"Looks like we survived again, then, huh?"*

Ari's soft fur was warm and comforting, and Birlerion's eyelids drooped. Had he dreamt speaking with Marguerite? He wasn't sure, but cocooned by his sentinal's concern and the little Arifel, he fell asleep.

Waking with a jerk, Birlerion realised that Ari had blinked out, back to his own endeavours no doubt, but Birlerion appreciated the visit. Taking a deep breath that made his chest twinge, Birlerion tried to get up. He paused, resting on the side of his bed, his hands gripping the edge as his head swam. A soft exclamation had him peering up. Marguerite stood before him, her hands on her hips. "What do you think you are doing? You don't have the strength to get up by yourself."

"You said I've been here for over a month. I should be healed by now."

"Your sentinal brought you back from the brink of death. That's no mean feat and certainly not an overnight job," Marguerite snapped, pushing him back onto the bed. "Why aren't you keeping him in bed?" she asked the air above her, scowling up at the sentinal that surrounded them.

Birlerion chuckled. "Because I told him not too. I want to get up." The air around him warmed, and a flush of energy rushed through his body. He straightened. "Only for a few minutes to look outside and breathe the fresh air." He shuddered as his words reminded him of the tragedy in Terolia, one of many memories and experiences he hadn't had time to process, and that still grated on his nerves.

Marguerite placed a hand on his chest. "I wasn't going to say anything yet, but you need to know what happened." The reluctance was clear in her voice as she sat next to him. "I'm sorry, Birlerion. There is no easy way to say this, but we lost some friends in that final battle."

Birlerion tensed as his heart raced in his aching chest.

Marguerite stroked his arm as his sentinal hummed with concern. "Tagerill, Versillion, and Marianille are all fine," she said in a rush, "but we lost Chryllion and Saerille."

The loss hit him, and Birlerion shuddered, his guts roiling

as he realised he would never see his friends again. "No," he whispered as their faces swam before his blurring eyes.

"I am so sorry," Marguerite said helplessly.

"Who else?" he asked, knowing there were more.

"Adilion."

Birlerion closed his eyes. No. Adilion had been one of his closest friends. They had been at the academy together.

"And Yaserille and Lorillion."

Birlerion's heart twisted, and he panted as his chest constricted and tears leaked down his cheeks.

"Their trees are on the plateau; you'll see them as soon as you go outside, along with Serillion's sentinal."

"I want to see them."

Marguerite heaved a sigh. "If you fall over, it won't be my fault," she said, though she helped him up and shoved her shoulder under his armpit to steady him. He wavered and then, stiffening, staggered to the edge of the room and out into the sunshine.

He inhaled. The scent of fresh grass and meadow flowers tickled his nose, and he sneezed. He held his chest as the ache spiked. Marguerite helped him to the bench and he thumped down with a groan as he tried to inhale again. His breath caught twice but still didn't grab enough air, and he concentrated on his breathing, in and out, until his rising panic subsided.

Marguerite tucked a blanket around his shoulders. The air had a chill bite to it, even though most of the snow had melted, leaving a slushy mire behind.

Releasing his grip on the bench, Birlerion looked around. A canvas tent stood beside his sentinal. The tall tree arched protectively over them, its silver bark glistening in the sunlight. A fire pit had been dug between them. The smoke from the crackling fire drifted in the still air and teased his nose with the scent of resin and burnt wood. The plains of

Oprimere stretched out before him: grassy knolls interspersed with slashes of deep brown soil, torn open to the sky. Ditches crisscrossed the plain, and discarded weapons glinted in the sunlight. Bright meadow flowers danced in the breeze, out of season and out of place in the war torn plain, but typical of Marguerite.

He scowled at the scene. "You haven't healed the land," he said, stilling as his gaze reached the raised plateau to the east. Six tall sentinal trees crowned the top, their silver trunks burnished by the golden sun.

"It will heal on its own. I thought you were more important. And anyway, I don't think that final confrontation should be forgotten so soon. Healing the scars will only hide the wounds; people need to understand and accept what happened. Many a pilgrim will come here, trying to find peace out of loss."

"True." There was a small silence. "Five. We lost five more."

"Yes."

Tears filled his eyes as their names chimed through him, all friends who would be much missed. "Doesn't seem real, does it?" he said, blindly staring at the sentinals. "If it wasn't for them, in time, all this would be forgotten."

Marguerite sat on the bench and gently embraced him. "It will never be forgotten."

"Of course it will. It will fade into history, much as it did the last time. The grass will grow," he smiled briefly, "if you allow it, and it will all become myth and legend." He held his chest and took a shallow breath before looking up at the brilliant blue sky. "Leyandrii's really gone this time, hasn't she?"

"She is still watching."

Birlerion smiled, crinkling the corner of his eyes. "Good."

2

By the end of the week, Birlerion could walk by himself to the plateau. The fact that he fell onto his bed every afternoon, exhausted, and slept until the next day was enough of a sign that he was still far from healed. It reminded him of his training sessions with Leyandrii all those centuries ago when she had taught him how to create his shield. He wondered if he had any power left but he was too exhausted to find out, too breathless, but not so much as before. The breathing exercises were helping.

Watching Taurillion practice in the weak sunshine had him alternating between wishing he could join him and frustration at how weak he felt. Taurillion oozed health. His skin was bronzed by the sun and his muscles were sleek and strong; he reeked of strength. Birlerion left Marguerite as she admired Taurillion's physique and took his pathetic body up to the plateau, where he collapsed against Serillion's tree.

The trunk warmed behind his back, and he patted the roots. "What a pair we are," he murmured, leaning his head back and peering up into the pointy leaves above. Tears sprang into his eyes, and he wiped them away in frustration at crying so easily. He missed his friend. He pictured his face, tousled blond hair above a thin, intelligent face; his gleaming grey eyes before they had turned silver. Quiet and bookish, he should have gone into the Chapterhouse and not the rangers. He might have lived his life in full if he had.

His thoughts drifted to Adilion, cheeky and irrepressible. His deep brown face appeared before him: broad forehead, wide mouth, blue-black curly hair bouncing around his grinning face. Adilion would tell him to get on with it, to stop brooding, and to live his life *for* them. He imagined Serillion peering over Adilion's shoulder, a knowing smile on his lips and saying: "You've done your dying. Make the most of the living."

Lips quirking, he used Serillion's tree to stand and then said his farewells, pausing at each tree: Adilion, Yaserille, Lorillion, Saerille, and Chryllion; all friends and much missed. He turned away and carefully slid down the bank; no point breaking a leg to add to his misery.

Shrugging off his melancholy thoughts, he joined Marguerite beside the fire. The sun was low in the sky. Streaks of red and orange muted the deepening blue, casting long shadows, which flickered in the firelight.

"Will they stay here?" he asked as he made himself comfortable on the rug.

"My arms will be around them always; they won't be alone," Marguerite replied as she stirred the pot hanging over the fire. "Keep an eye on that for me, will you?" she asked, and then she rose and walked to her tent.

Birlerion rubbed his fingers together, idly watching the fire. Nothing. He twisted his wrist, compressing the air. Nothing. No heat, no sparkle, no magic. He was ordinary at last. He wouldn't be expected to shield anyone against anything; he was no different to any other soldier.

Leaning forward, he stirred the pot, rapping the spoon against the edge before resting it across the top. He glanced around the little campsite; he was alone. Marguerite and Taurillion were busy elsewhere. He looked at his hands. They should be busy, cleaning his sword, making arrows, cleaning tack. Cleaning tack—his breath caught at the thought. According to Maraine, the Medera of the Atolea, his Darian stallion was waiting for him in Greens. What was he doing languishing here? He needed to go and get him. His Darian had been waiting for far too long.

Tomorrow, he would begin training in earnest, no matter what Marguerite said; it was time to go home. Stirring the pot again, he inhaled the fragrant aroma as he wondered where the others had gone but didn't pursue the thought. He didn't blame them; they had been parted for over three thousand years, after all. Swinging the pot off the heat, he rose. They would turn up eventually. He would make a start on his arrows.

Birlerion had added more water to the stew twice before they joined him by the fire. Damp and fresh-faced, they had found a river to dip in, which was quite a nice thought; he could do with a bath. His quiver was full, and he had moved on to curing the skin of the rabbit he had caught. His sack of stones had been replenished as well, and his sling arm seemed to have fully recovered, as had his eye.

"I've eaten, so help yourselves," he said as he dunked the rabbit skin in a pot of salty water and left it to steep. He wiped his hands and returned to his rug as an owl hooted in the distance, the mournful sound carrying on the night air.

"We ought to be thinking about going home," Birlerion said once Taurillion had sat down with his bowl.

Taurillion flicked a glance at him. "And where is home?"

"For me? Greens. For you?" Birlerion shrugged. "You tell me."

"Wherever Marguerite is."

Marguerite's lips curved into a self-satisfied smile. "We'll be staying in Elothia. Taurillion needs to return to Randolf, and I have much to do."

"Will Leyandrii return?" asked Birlerion. "One day?"

"We must pray so, but in the meantime, we will keep Remargaren safe between us."

"It will be weird not rushing from one crisis to the next. I'm surprised no one's been by to chase us down."

"I told them to stay away. No point visiting while you were unconscious, and you needed time to work your way back."

"Do you wish you had gone with Leyandrii? Wherever she went?"

"No, I had plenty of reasons to stay here. One of us had to stay; otherwise, who would be keeping an eye on you, Birlerion?"

"When I woke, I thought I was back then; you know, the first time around."

"I know." Marguerite's voice was soft. "I'm sorry, Birlerion."

Taurillion glanced at him. "Talking about the first time, you didn't need to face the Ascendants alone that night in Vespers. You could have come with me. Why didn't you?"

Birlerion twisted his lips. "Leyandrii knew there was a communications array in the building; she could sense the dead air. But the only way to make the Ascendants concentrate on Leyandrii was for Clary to see me. It was the only way to make him commit everything. He wouldn't be able to resist. He had to think he could wipe us all out in one go. But I couldn't protect Leyandrii *and* the people."

"You were never meant to, Birlerion," Marguerite said. "You did what you were supposed to. You protected her people; she couldn't have asked for more. She couldn't stay once the Veil had descended, and Guerlaire chose to go with her."

"Where did they go?" Birlerion asked as he threw another stick on the fire and watched the sparks fly. He thought about the woman who had ensnared him, heart and soul: Leyandrii, the deity who had protected Remargaren with her life; Marguerite's sister.

"There are many other worlds out there. Some, the Mother created. Others existed before the Mother. She watches over them all. There is a lot of space beyond the Veil, but for now, it shields us, keeps us safe. You and Jerrol made sure of that."

"Yes, we did it all over again. How is Jerrol?"

"Better than you. As is Tagerill. They are both back on duty, Jerrol with the king and Tagerill in Deepwater with Jennery."

"Good." Birlerion breathed a silent sigh of relief that his brother Tagerill was well.

They fell into a comfortable silence. The fire crackling made him jump. His eyes had been drooping, and he stirred himself to go to bed.

The next morning, he was up early and staggering around the plateau; he couldn't really call it running. When Taurillion appeared, Birlerion persuaded him to let him spar until he collapsed, which, unfortunately, didn't take very long, and then Marguerite came rushing up, scolding both him and Taurillion for overdoing it.

"I won't improve if I don't push myself," Birlerion gasped, trying to catch his breath.

"No more today. Sit by your sentinal and don't move," Marguerite snapped as Taurillion helped him stand. He wheezed, struggling to drag in a breath as Taurillion held him.

"Marguerite, we hardly started. We sparred for maybe half a chime, nothing. He shouldn't be this exhausted."

Marguerite huffed in frustration. "What did you expect? You fools. His chest was crushed. His *lungs* collapsed; he stopped *breathing*. He has to retrain his body to cope. It takes time; much longer than healing broken bones. It will take months."

Birlerion stirred in Taurillion's arms. "Months? It can't take months."

"Months," Marguerite reiterated, "which is why I will be going with you when you travel to Greens. I don't trust you to be sensible."

Birlerion was a shadow of himself the following day. He sat under his tree, watching the day progress, unnaturally pale and subdued. His chest ached, a deep, dark ache that told him how close to death he had been. He was suitably chastised, and Marguerite watched him thoughtfully.

A flicker in the air preceded the arrival of Ari, the small Arifel; a fluffy, kitten-like creature with scaly wings and tail, mackerel-coloured striped fur, white chest and toes. He hovered in front of Birlerion and meeped mournfully. Birlerion extended his hand, and the little Arifel landed, crouched in his palm and crooned at him.

Birlerion smoothed a finger down his chest, and the Arifel rubbed his head against his hand. Vivid images of rocky pools and sunny ledges filled his mind, along with the image of a black and white Arifel. Her name popped into his head, Lin, and Ari preened.

"Your mate?" he thought. *"Congratulations."*

Another flurry of images had Birlerion chuckling: tiny fluffy bundles of fur. *"Ari, you are a fast worker. Congratulations again."*

Ari crooned and tilted his head at Marguerite, his green eyes growing larger as he stared at her. She extended her hand, and her face softened as she accepted the images. At his news, her face brightened.

"If there is no magic, how did he manage that?" Birlerion asked with a laugh.

"I imagine he timed it perfectly," she replied, giving the little Arifel his instructions. He chittered at Birlerion and vanished.

Marguerite stood. "Come on. Let's go for a walk. You need the exercise." Birlerion grimaced but rose and joined her.

He was panting again by the time they returned, and he dropped to the rug. "Marguerite, there has to be something you can do to help. I can't go on like this."

"I'm sorry, Birlerion. Your sentinal has done all he can. There's nothing I can do. Time is a great healer. You will just have to be patient."

Birlerion huffed as he lay down and stared at the sky. "Months," he said under his breath. He peered up at Marguerite. "How long are you able to stay? I thought you said you needed to go with Taurillion to Elothia and fix some stuff?" She was, after all, bonded with the land. She was the deity that kept their world together.

"For you, it can wait."

"As much as I appreciate your support, why, Marguerite? I'm just one of Leyandrii's Sentinals; one of many."

Marguerite's face grew solemn. She glanced at the plateau. "One of a dwindling number, and Birlerion, you know you are different. It's not something that was spoken of, but Leyandrii always had her eye on you. Without my sister here ... well, I'm the next best thing."

"You mean something else is expected of me," he said, leaning his head back and staring up at the sky.

"I don't know, but you are the shield, and as long as there is a Captain to be the sword, the shield will be needed.

Birlerion, don't get fixated on that. Concentrate on yourself. You can't help Jerrol until you fully recover, and you are certainly not returning to duty until I say so."

Birlerion glanced at Marguerite. "I need to go to Greens, sooner rather than later. Someone is waiting for me; impatiently, I might add."

"I forgot about him." She stared at him for a moment. "Maybe it is for the best. He will be a good tonic for you; a much-needed boost." She nodded to herself. "Yes, it's time to relocate to Greens. I'll speak to your sentinal. You can't travel by waystone; he'll have to take you."

"What?" Birlerion jerked upright. "Why can't I travel by waystone?"

"Your chest won't survive the pressure. You are healed, yes, but the repairs are fragile until the bone strengthens. What happened to you was no normal injury. An Ascendant lord blasted you with all his power; it is a miracle you are alive. In fact, I'm not sure *how* you are alive. You shouldn't be. So Birlerion, please, don't make it more difficult than it has to be."

Birlerion sat back, stunned. "I didn't realise how bad it was."

"I know. There was no point in telling you, but you need to be careful. As I said, it will take time. Please let it, Birlerion."

"I'll try," Birlerion said slowly. "But you know what my life has been like. I don't seem to get the choice. I've almost died so many times it amazes me I'm still here, ready to be battered again. Do you think there will ever be a time when I can live just for me? Have a life of my own?"

Marguerite knelt before him and cupped his gaunt face in her hands. "I hope so. You deserve one. Know that I will always be at your side, and if I can help, I will." She kissed his cheek and grinned at him. "I'll look out for a suitable young lady for you. It seems to be the season for it."

"That I will do for myself."

Marguerite tilted her head. "Well, if you're sure, but I'll keep a lookout all the same. I always thought young Kayerille would be a good match. I know you two get on well."

Birlerion stared at her, horrified. "Don't you dare, Marguerite. She's a good friend of mine. Don't spoil it."

3

The next morning, Birlerion was seated outside his sentinal, dutifully being careful. He was fast concluding that he couldn't live his life being careful; he just wasn't made that way. Maybe that was why the Lady had chosen him as her shield. He couldn't sit still for one morning, let alone months. Maybe that was a prerequisite for being a Sentinal; the inability to sit still.

He brightened as the waystone chimed. Visitors.

He stood, more to give the impression that he was fine than for any other reason, and a wide grin spread over his face as he saw who was approaching: a tall, thin Sentinal with a broadsword on his back, accompanied by a slight, brown-haired man; the current Lady's Captain. Birlerion engulfed the smaller man in a hug. "Jerrol, what brings you here? Niallerion, it's so good to see you."

"By the Lady, I'm so glad to see you standing. Birlerion, you frightened the life out of us." Niallerion gripped Birlerion's arms and inspected him. He grimaced at what he saw, obviously concerned.

"Let's sit," Jerrol suggested, his eyes raking his friend with keen scrutiny. "We were worried about you. Ari only just told us you were conscious. We came as soon as we heard."

"Are *you* all right? I don't remember much at the end," Birlerion said as he sat.

Jerrol grimaced. "I'm not surprised. It was chaos. I'm fine. You sheltered me, and the Lady did the rest. I think maybe you came off worse. I am sorry, Birlerion. I had no idea what was going to happen."

Birlerion shrugged. "Hazard of the job." As he tilted his head to inspect Jerrol, he observed how Jerrol's skin glistened in the sunlight like twinkling crystal. "I would suggest you didn't come away completely unaffected."

"No, the Bloodstone left its mark."

"And the Veil," Birlerion murmured.

Jerrol cast him a sharp glance. "Yes, you would know about that, wouldn't you?"

Niallerion frowned at them, at a loss. "How are you, Birlerion? When can we expect you back?"

"Not for a good month, if not longer," Marguerite said from behind them.

Niallerion lurched to his feet, and a broad smile spread across his face. "Marguerite, how long have you been here?"

"Since Birlerion needed me," she replied, returning his hug.

Jerrol slowly stood. "You're real," he said, stupefied, as the auburn-haired deity patted his face.

"Of course I'm real." She cast a glance at Birlerion and sat next to him.

Niallerion sank to the ground, his face wreathed in smiles. "Is Taurillion here?"

"He's around somewhere. Someone has to keep Birlerion in order."

Niallerion glanced at Birlerion, uncertain, and Birlerion grinned. "I needed a sparring partner."

Jerrol sat. "But how are you here? You are the Land."

"I am Remargaren, and when her protectors need assistance, I respond. Birlerion protected us and suffered for it. I will do what I can to help him recover. Leyandrii managed to protect you, and you seem to have come out better than expected."

Jerrol shrugged. "I'm not sure I would say that. I must admit, the world appears different now, and the Veil ... it calls."

"Ignore it," Birlerion and Marguerite said together.

"More easily said than done," Jerrol said.

"A matter of willpower and the knowledge that the Veil will consume you if you let it. Never trust it," Birlerion said, his face grave.

"What he said," Marguerite said with a grin as Taurillion approached with a bottle of white wine and some glasses in his hands.

Jerrol glanced across at the sentinal trees on the plateau. "I do understand the threat. After all, look at what Ellaerion and Elliarille suffered. They still recover in their trees in Marchwood. We were lucky to save them. Lorillion got tangled up in us and couldn't let go."

"He always was tenacious," Birlerion replied, and left it at that.

As Taurillion poured the wine, Niallerion filled Birlerion in on what had happened to everyone in the final battle on the plateau.

"How is Lord Jason? Sounds like Stoneford came off worst," Birlerion commented at the end.

"He feels it keenly," Jerrol admitted. "I assigned Darllion to him, but it's not the same."

"I hear you finally got your own sentinal tree. Took you long enough, though I expect the king will want his courtyard back." Birlerion chuckled at the thought, and he tried to disguise the wheeze as he inhaled.

Jerrol cast him a worried glance. "Yes, Taelia was quite surprised. By the way, she can't wait to see you. She is worried about you. I should warn you, she's a bit excitable at the moment. The Lady granted her eyesight, and everything and everyone is very new."

"Add to that the fact that she is increasing and Jerrol is trying to find them a family home," Niallerion interjected.

Jerrol flushed at Birlerion's effusive congratulations. "I know, I know. I want to go back to Stoneford, but the king wants me in Vespers."

"Why can't you have both?" Birlerion suggested. "You could create a waystone in your sentinal; only you would be able to use it. Would take you moments to travel."

Jerrol raised his eyebrows. "I could? I thought it would be open to all."

"Depends on how you create it. But if you work with your sentinal, he would only allow entry to those you grant permission."

"Well, that solves that problem, then. I'm glad I came." He scowled at Niallerion. "Why didn't you tell me?"

Niallerion shrugged his narrow shoulders. "I don't know everything, you know."

"We need you back, Birlerion," said Jerrol. "*I* need you back. We have much rebuilding to do, and I could use your help."

"You'll have to wait," Marguerite warned. "He has only been awake for a week, and he is still recuperating."

Birlerion was glad that she didn't say more, but he was exhausted, and all he had been doing was talking. His chest was tight. He centred himself for a moment, concentrating on his breathing. His sentinal hummed in concern, and he relaxed as the tree's gentle embrace infused him with a flush of warmth.

Kneeling by the fire, Taurillion dug out a stone cylinder from the pit and dished up dinner. The aroma of rich rabbit stew made their mouths water, and the conversation moved on to the king's latest projects.

"When will you be well enough to travel to Greens?" Jerrol asked.

"We were discussing that earlier," said Birlerion. "I can recuperate there just as well as here. Better, I expect, and if Maraine is correct, my Darian still awaits me."

"Good. I'm sorry we didn't get the chance to return earlier." Jerrol pushed his hair out of his eyes with a rueful expression on his face. "Events kept overtaking us."

"It wasn't your fault," Birlerion replied, shying away from the more painful memories.

At the bleak expression on Birlerion's face, Niallerion changed the subject. "Your tree is missed in Vespers. The temple doesn't look right without him."

"Why don't you relocate yours? No one will know the difference. It will be a while before we return to Vespers," Birlerion said, staring across at his sentinal.

"It doesn't seem right," Niallerion said, "and you'd be surprised how many would notice."

There wasn't much more to say after that, and Jerrol rose. "We look forward to your return. You are missed, Birlerion, by all of us. Take care of him." He grinned at Marguerite, still amazed to see her in the flesh.

"Oh, don't worry. I will."

Niallerion escorted Jerrol back to the waystone, and Birlerion raised a hand in farewell as they shimmered out of sight. The peace of the plateau descended once more, oppressive and silent. Birlerion gave Marguerite a brief hug and went to bed.

A week later, Birlerion relaxed in his sentinal and allowed it to spin its golden strands around him. The sentinal's hum filled his mind, and he merged with his tree, lost in its exuberant embrace.

Marguerite watched the tall sentinal shudder. The long, pointy leaves rustled overhead before an unexpected flash of golden light caressed the sentinals on the plateau in farewell. Then he shimmered out of sight, leaving a slight depression in the ground as the only sign that he had ever been there.

4

L ord Simeon of Greenswatch gripped the edge of his desk as the building trembled. As the tremors stilled, he lurched to his feet, his heart pounding.

"Frenerion, what was that?"

The stocky Sentinal guarding his door grinned at the young lord. "At a guess, I would say a sentinal just arrived."

"A sentinal? Whose?"

Frenerion shrugged. "I'd have to go and see, but Birlerion's springs to mind. He's been stuck in Oprimere for weeks."

"Why come here? Wouldn't he return to Vespers?"

"You'd have to ask him," Frenerion said, his silver eyes gleaming.

"Then let's do that," Simeon replied, leading the way around the manor house to the homefield, where Versillion's sentinal tree stood. When they arrived, a crowd of servants and off duty guards were staring up at the second graceful tree now standing in the field. A broad-shouldered Sentinal, Frenerion's age but with a shock of deep-red hair, stood with his hand on the trunk.

"Versillion, is it Birlerion's?" Simeon asked as he reached the Sentinal.

"Yes, and it seems Birlerion travelled with him. He sleeps. I hope he is alright. Why would he risk travelling now?"

Simeon inspected the sentinal tree. It was taller than Versillion's, and the trunk sparkled as if flecked with glass as it settled. The deep-green canopy rustled, and Versillion's sentinal responded.

Versillion grinned. "He's come home to recuperate."

"Well, he is welcome. I must admit, he has more chance of resting here than Vespers." Simeon's eyes widened. "He's here for his Darian, isn't he? What do we tell him?"

"Nothing yet. Let's see how he is first." Versillion tilted his head, a crease between his brows. "I don't think he is well."

"What? How can you tell?"

"His sentinal is worried."

Simeon stared harder at the tree, but it looked the same as Versillion's to him. "Inform me when he wakes. Whatever he needs, he is welcome to. I'll inform Healer Liria her services may be needed."

"Thank you, my lord," Versillion murmured, his attention still firmly on his brother's tree.

"Everyone else, back to work. You'll meet him soon enough." Simeon's command had his people scattering.

"He won't wake until his sentinal lets him, and his sentinal is cautious," Marguerite said, and Versillion spun in surprise. Frenerion gasped from behind Simeon.

Versillion's face lit up, and he stooped to hug her. "Marguerite, where did you come from?"

"Oof. Put me down, you brute. You don't know your own strength. Taurillion and I have been keeping an eye on Birlerion"

"Is Taurillion with you?" Versillion peered around him, as if expecting the other Sentinal to suddenly appear.

"No, he went back to Retarfu to join the grand duke."

"It's so good to see you. We thought you were lost with the Lady." Frenerion had snuck around to hug her too, and she laughed, pleased.

Simeon gawped at the beautiful young woman dwarfed by his Sentinals as she patted Frenerion's arm. "No, I am still here. Birlerion needed me."

"Is he alright?" Versillion asked.

"No, not really." Marguerite sighed and then smiled at the shocked lord of Greenswatch. "Lord Simeon, my apologies for not warning you that we were coming. I never thought. We were more concerned about getting Birlerion here in one piece."

"Of c-course. You are more than welcome," he stuttered.

"What's wrong with Birlerion, Marguerite?" asked Versillion. "I thought he was recovering well. That's what Niallerion said."

"He's being himself, trying to do too much too fast."

Versillion chuckled. "And you are surprised?"

"No, I suppose not. I'm hoping his Darian will be a calming influence. Bonding should keep him quiet for a while."

"Ah, about that," said Simeon. "His Darian isn't here. We weren't going to say anything yet, but we had some trouble a couple of weeks ago. He was stolen."

"What? By whom?"

Simeon spread his hands and stared down at his boots. "We don't know. There was a fire in the stables. We know now that it was a diversion, but at the time, and in the confusion of saving the horses, someone nabbed him. It wasn't until the next morning that he was discovered missing. We sent men down the East Road to the border, but there were no reports of him. He is quite distinctive, being honey gold in colour. Quite unusual. You'd expect someone to have seen him."

"If someone is determined, they will find a way," said Marguerite. "Who would have known he was here? The agreement is between Greens and the Atolea. I didn't think it was public knowledge."

Simeon looked around. "If Birlerion is not going to wake soon, maybe we ought to go inside and have this conversation."

Versillion patted Birlerion's tree. "He'll tell us when Birlerion is ready to wake." He tucked Marguerite's arm in his and escorted her towards the house. "Why didn't you use the waystone? Why is he in a deep sleep?"

"He isn't strong enough. You forget his rib cage was crushed—not broken, crushed. The power it took to do that was phenomenal. What his sentinal has done to heal him is beyond comprehension, but it takes time. He won't be able to use the waystone for months; not until his bone density improves. His sentinal immersed him so he could buffer the effect of the transition."

"Immersed?"

Marguerite hesitated, climbing the steps into the house before answering. "Similar to the sleep you all experienced."

"Will he fully recover?" Versillion asked, dropping his voice.

"I don't know." Versillion's breath hitched, and Marguerite turned to him and patted his arm. "He gets disoriented, confused as to which time he is in, which is to be expected, but it catches him out; he finds it distressing." Marguerite bit her lip. "I think the two events have merged into one for him; both traumatic, both life-threatening."

"None of us really know what he did, or what he suffered as a result. Surely, Leyandrii—"

"Versillion. Don't you think we've all done what we can?" Marguerite peered up at him.

"Of course, I'm sorry." Versillion rubbed a hand over his face.

"Don't be. We're all concerned. He is important to all of us. I promise."

"Please make yourselves comfortable," Simeon said, motioning them into the drawing room. He paused to speak to the footmen in the corridor before joining them.

"For Birlerion," said Versillion, "it would be like losing his family all over again, and he fought so hard to get one in the first place. It means even more to him."

"Which is why we brought him home. He has a connection to Greens. I thought it might help, and the Darian was a bonus. If he were here," she said with a twist of her lips.

Simeon grimaced. "Think of all those months we didn't even know he was here. My father never said anything; only he and our horse master, George, knew. It wasn't until I took over the guardianship that George came and told me.

"He showed me the agreement and the stallion. Once in a generation, a Darian would be brought to Greens for the lord to hold for Birlerion and, if not claimed within a decade, could do with it as he wished. Now that I know, I can't believe we never recognised him for what he was. He was beautiful; a rich honey gold with a black mane and tail. Exquisite."

"What happened to those that were never claimed?" Frenerion asked. "Aren't all Darians supposed to bond?"

"From what I can tell, they either bonded with someone else or were returned to the Atolea."

"Even though the agreement was for Greens to use them at their will?"

"I don't know." Simeon pursed his lips. "In all these years, you'd think our stable would only be Darians, but this was the first in our generation. George, though, seems to know all about them. It was almost as if he was expecting the Darian to arrive. My father must have told him about the agreement with the Atolea."

"When did he arrive, my lord?" Frenerion asked.

"According to George, last Sepu. A son of the Atolea bought him. Birlerion hasn't been back since."

"Birlerion had no idea that a Darian was waiting for him until he went to Terolia with Jerrol and the Atolea told him," said Marguerite. "After the Watch Towers and Oprimere, he hasn't had a chance to return until now. If their paths hadn't crossed, neither would know."

"So, Birlerion won't be able to track him?"

"I have no idea. I doubt it, but we would have to ask him." Marguerite leaned forward. "He might. He knew the Darian was impatient. Whether that was intuition or not, I don't know."

"Knowing Birlerion, it's a difficult call to make. My brother constantly surprises us," Versillion murmured.

"So, we wait for Birlerion to wake up," Simeon said, accepting the glass from the manservant.

"But the Darian will be long gone," Frenerion objected.

"He already is. We have no idea where he is," Simeon said, taking a sip of his wine. "How long before Birlerion wakes?"

"I'm not sure. Tomorrow at the earliest, I think," Marguerite said.

"I'll wait for him in my sentinal," said Versillion. "He'll know. It will be best if Birlerion sees me first, especially if you think he'll be disoriented."

"Very well. Until then, Lady Marguerite, may we offer you a room? There's time to bathe before dinner. Whatever Greens can offer is yours."

Marguerite's smile lit up her face. "A bath would be

wonderful. It has been many years since I stayed here. The hospitality of Greens was legendary."

"Well, we'll have to be on our mettle, then."

"I wouldn't worry. Any descendant of Warren's will be perfectly capable," Marguerite reassured him. "And you have Versillion to guide you. I'm sure you can't go wrong."

When Birlerion opened his eyes, he knew he was in Greens. He felt it in his bones. His sentinal was a comforting hum in the back of his mind, wrapping around him like a protective blanket. He sat up. He was home.

The sentinal released him, withdrawing but still present. They were closer now than they had ever been, and Birlerion felt comforted by his presence. The sentinal had kept him alive and would continue to do so, and Birlerion knew that they were so enmeshed they would never truly separate. It was a reassuring thought.

He swung his legs over his bed and took a breath. His chest still ached, but it was more of an echo, one he could ignore. The thought of seeing his parents had him rising. He needed to speak to Warren.

Shimmering out of the sentinal, he paused for a moment to adjust to the brilliant sunlight. He was surrounded by shades of green; the open field, the surrounding trees. He frowned over the unfamiliar lake, the ranks of evergreens, the grassy lawn leading to the back of the house. Climbing roses crawled up the trellis against the grey stone wall and pots of flowers sat on the terrace.

Melis had been busy. He didn't remember it being so colourful.

"Birlerion, finally. I thought you were going to sleep all week."

Birlerion's heart thumped, and he grinned as he reached out to hug his brother. "As if. You know perfectly well Pa would be chasing me down the stairs. Bed is for slackers or the injured; there is too much to do to be wasting it lying down. You can do that when you're dead."

"True, though you have been ill. Pa would have given you a pass," Versillion said, watching his brother carefully.

Easing his shoulders, Birlerion grimaced. "I need to speak to Pa. Clary attacked me again."

Versillion tightened his grip on Birlerion's arms. He was too thin, and there was a breathiness about his voice that wasn't right. "Birlerion, I am so sorry. Pa isn't here. I know you just woke up, but your sentinal brought you from the plateau at Oprimere yesterday."

Birlerion stiffened in confusion. Oprimere? That couldn't be right. His sentinal crooned, and his creeping distress eased as Versillion continued. "You were injured protecting Jerrol. Birlerion, it is 4125, and Marguerite is here with you. Simeon is lord of Greens."

Birlerion jerked back, and Versillion stepped forward, keeping hold of him. "What? No. Where are Warren and Melis?"

Tears sprang into Versillion's eyes, and he hugged his brother tight. "They are lost in time, Birlerion. Safe in our hearts and memories but no longer here."

Birlerion struggled in his brother's grip as grief rushed through him, but Versillion held him easily. No, they couldn't be gone; solid, reassuring Warren and Melis, always ready to welcome him home with open arms and a huge smile. Birlerion stopped struggling as he remembered, and he shuddered as he hid his face in Versillion's shoulder.

"It's alright. You're safe in Greens. She hasn't forgotten you," Versillion murmured in his ear.

"I'm sorry," Birlerion gasped, his chest wheezing in his distress. "I'm so sorry. I thought ... I thought ..."

"I know. I've got you. You're home now."

Birlerion lifted his face as he got his emotions under control, and Versillion winced at the sight of his brother's eyes. The shine of tears made them molten silver, enough to drown in. He led Birlerion into his sentinal and sat him down. Handing him a glass of water the sentinal had procured for him, he wrung out a cloth and offered it to his brother.

Birlerion wiped his face. Folding the cloth, he pressed the cool material against his eyes. "I'm sorry," he murmured.

Versillion crouched beside Birlerion, his face mirroring his concern. "You have no need to be. They loved you just as much as you loved them; there is no shame in that. You're home now, and we need to get you better. You are whistling like a steam kettle."

"I can't seem to get enough air. Sometimes it's difficult to breathe."

"A result of putting your lungs through the wringer. I didn't realise you took so much damage. Marguerite is up at the house with Simeon. She has been filling us in."

A faint smile flickered over Birlerion's lips. "She won't let me do anything."

"For good reason. Greens will help. With fresh air, good food, and excellent company, you'll soon improve. Your sentinal is amazing. We are lucky to have you here." Versillion offered Birlerion another cloth. "Your face is blotchy. Can't have a son of Greens looking such a mess."

Birlerion chuckled and dabbed at his face. "It's good to be home." He sipped his water and sighed. His head ached, but, his sentinal soon smoothed it away.

Versillion wrinkled his brow as he listened to his sentinal. "What happened then?"

"When?"

"Just now. My sentinal said there was a ripple from your sentinal."

"Oh, he got rid of my headache."

Versillion clamped his lips shut. Birlerion didn't seem to think anything of it, but that wasn't normal. Sentinals didn't reach; you had to be touching them for them to heal. "Simeon is waiting to see you when you're ready. And Frenerion."

"I suppose we'd better go in, then. Isn't it great that Marguerite is here?" Birlerion twisted his lips. "Though, with the Veil well and truly sealed, Leyandrii won't be able to reach us."

"Not something we want to bandy about too much. The people won't understand. They'll think She's deserted them," Versillion said.

"It's no different from the last time. She's not been physically here for centuries, but Her reach extends farther than you think. She'll keep us busy."

"That's good, then," Versillion said as he rose. "Ready?"

Birlerion stood, and they left the sentinal. Versillion wrapped his arm around Birlerion's shoulders, and they walked up to the house.

5

F renerion met them in the entrance hall. "Birlerion."
He hugged his friend. "Lad, what have you been
doing to yourself? You need to get out in the sun; the
washed-out look does not suit you."

"Thanks, I think," Birlerion replied as Frenerion opened
a door and ushered him in.

Versillion's face creased with concern as he watched
Birlerion cross the room to greet Lord Simeon.

Birlerion smiled as he extended his hand, but it didn't lift
the strain on his face. "Lord Simeon. It is so nice to be
home."

"Welcome, Birlerion. I think Greens is happy to see you.
Please, sit. How are you? I must admit, I can't get over seeing
a second sentinal in the homefield. They are so mesmerising;
they catch your eye without trying. I count us doubly fortunate to have the original sons of Greens here with us." He
missed Versillion's wince at the reminder that his eldest
brother was long dead and would never be with them at
Greens again, and continued. "Honestly, Birlerion, if there is
anything we can do for you, anything at all, please let me
know."

"Thank you, my lord. I appreciate it."

"I know you are still recuperating. Our healer is available should you need her."

"My sentinal watches over me. He will keep me standing. I am improving, it just takes time to recover from such an injury." Birlerion smiled to detract from the seriousness of his words.

"Good, good." Simeon glanced at Versillion and then back to Birlerion. "I am afraid I have some unfortunate news for you. There is no point sugar-coating it, and someone will blurt it out anyway. We had a fire in the stables a couple of weeks ago, and in the confusion, your Darian was stolen."

Birlerion's breath caught on a wheeze. "But he is alright? He wasn't injured?" He tugged at his collar as it suddenly felt tight. His mind spun. Kin'arol wasn't here? He hadn't realised how much he was depending on his Darian to help him to recover.

"As far as we know. We think the fire was just a diversion. It wasn't serious, but horses don't react well to smoke. The thing is, we haven't been able to find him. We sent men up the East Road to the border with Terolia and up through the borders to Elothia, but there were no sightings of him in either direction."

"We were just discussing who knew he was here," Marguerite said as Birlerion tried to relax in his chair. He breathed deliberately, and the wheeze eased.

Birlerion took a deeper, steadying breath. He glanced around the room, feeling on edge. "The Atolean wouldn't steal him back, though many Terolians dislike the fact that Darians are being sent out of the Family's control."

"But you are Family," Marguerite objected.

"Few know that. I'd be seen as a heathen, an outsider. Greens is not of the Family. Resentment builds in the oddest of places."

"True, and unchecked, it can build over time, and they've had centuries," Simeon said.

"I doubt this resentment is that old. If it is Terolian, then I expect if anyone had a gripe and wanted to get back at the Atolean, it would be Kirshan."

"Why Kirshan?" Versillion asked.

"Because when Jerrol annexed Terolia for Benedict, he exposed the Kirshan leaders. He revealed that they were enspelled by *Mentiserium*, and as a result Maraine proposed the motion to remove them. The Kirshans are in disarray, leaderless until the next Medera is selected. And that could take months." Birlerion shifted in his seat, trying to relieve the discomfort that was slowly constricting his chest.

"But how does stealing your Darian affect the Atolea? Surely, Greens is at fault for allowing it to happen?" Simeon asked.

"According to the agreement between Tiv'erna and Warren a Darian should be here, waiting for me to bond with it. If there is no Darian to bond with me, then the Atolea default on their agreement with Greens."

"But I wouldn't enforce that. It's my fault, not theirs. They delivered the Darian to Greens as promised," Simeon said.

"Not in the eyes of the Families. There is no Darian here now, is there? The Kirshans could call Maraine before the conclave. They could force her to stand down. A Medera whose word cannot be trusted is no leader."

There was a small silence, and Birlerion tried to breathe shallowly. His chest wheezed from all the talking; it sounded loud in his ears, and from the way everyone was staring at him, they heard it too. "Family politics," he said. His breath caught at the back of his throat, and he succumbed to a coughing fit. He couldn't drag in enough air, and the room tilted as his vision blurred, greying around the edges until he collapsed.

"Breathe, Birlerion. Control it." Marguerite's voice was warm in his ear, as was his sentinal's hum. He was propped up on the floor against Versillion, who held him tightly. Simeon watched him, aghast, as Marguerite wiped his mouth. Crimson spots blotted the cloth, and his breath shuddered out as his body shook. Pain spiked through his chest.

A young woman knelt beside him. "It will soothe your throat and suppress the cough," she said. "Give you time to catch your breath." She tipped liquid in his mouth, and he choked it down. It burned on its way down, but he stopped coughing long enough to drag in some air, and he closed his eyes.

Someone with cool hands felt his forehead and cheeks and then gripped his wrist, and a low conversation continued around him. He was too exhausted to pay attention, and the next thing he knew, Versillion had picked him up and was carrying him out of the room.

"I can walk," he said, opening his eyes, but Versillion ignored him and strode up the stairs. Versillion helped him undress and forced him into bed.

"Rest, Birlerion. The healer will be here in a minute."

"I can't rest. We need to go to Terolia."

"We will when you're better."

"It might be too late. At least send a warning to Maraine. Don't let her be caught by surprise."

"I will. I promise. Now, stop fretting and do what the healer says."

Birlerion sighed and closed his eyes. "This is ridiculous," he murmured, but he dozed off under Versillion's concerned gaze.

When the healer arrived, he was fast asleep, and he didn't wake as she listened to his chest.

"Could you stay with him?"

"Of course," Versillion replied. "What's wrong?"

"Call me if his breathing changes in any way. I want to speak further with Lady Marguerite, but I think he has an infection."

Birlerion didn't remember much of the following week. The deep rumble of Warren's voice kept him company and comforted him, and he had long conversations with him. He had so much he wanted to tell him when they weren't forcing him to drink draughts that made him sleep. He hated being medicated, but he was too weak to stop them, and they ignored his protests.

It was a bright, sunny morning when he finally opened his eyes and the room no longer spun, and for once, he was alone. He took a deep breath, and his eyes widened as he finally felt like he was breathing properly and not at half-strength.

He turned his head as the door opened and Marguerite peered in. "Good morning."

"Hi," he whispered.

She came and sat beside him. "I'm so sorry, Birlerion."

His brow creased as he considered her words. "For what?"

"For missing the infection. I should have known from how difficult you were finding it to breathe, but I thought it was your lungs developing the strength to cope. It is fortunate that we came here; Liria specialises in respiration. You were lucky."

"About time I had some luck."

"True, but the good news is that the infection is treated and you should recover a lot faster now—*if* you do as she says. I mean it, Birlerion."

"I always do what I'm told," he said, and Marguerite let

out a shout of laughter. She was so vivacious and full of life that just watching her exhausted him.

"Versillion is getting some sleep. He'll be in later. He's been with you virtually all the time. You responded to him best; his presence soothed you, reassured you, I think."

Birlerion blushed. "I thought he was Warren." He raised a shaky hand to his face. His skin was smooth; Versillion must have shaved him. He closed his eyes. How embarrassing.

"I expect you to eat all of your breakfast. You have to eat well and put on some of the weight you've lost. Then you can start training." As his face brightened, Marguerite smiled, and when the tray arrived, he ate it without protest.

Versillion arrived with Birlerion's evening meal, and his face eased as he saw his brother sitting up and reading a book. "You look much better."

Birlerion grinned. "I feel much better, and I can actually breathe properly. It makes a huge difference." He rubbed his chin. "Thanks for the shave," he said, flushing.

"Any time," Versillion said lightly. He slid the tray on Birlerion's lap, and they chatted about Greens as Birlerion attacked his dinner with a healthy appetite.

The next day, Simeon came to visit. "You scared us half to death, Birlerion. I am thankful Liria was here. Otherwise, we wouldn't have known what to do with you."

"The Lady watches," Birlerion said with a small smile.

"That She does," Simeon agreed devoutly.

The following week, Birlerion was allowed as far as the sofa in the drawing room. He chuckled as Versillion sat opposite him. "This reminds me of the first time I arrived at Greens and your dog almost ate me. Penner had to haul him off me. He was the size of a small pony."

Versillion grinned. "That was the stupidest dog we ever owned. Tage loved him, though."

"He did. Penner did well, didn't he? When you look around Greens, it isn't that much different, really."

"Indeed, he managed to pass down the love of the land and the forests. Not the red hair, it seems, but most of the important stuff."

Birlerion laughed. "You and Tage will have to bring it back."

"Too late for that, I think. We'll have to give Greens a pass."

"Rubbish, you're not that much older than me; there is still plenty of time."

The next day, Birlerion graduated to the dining table, where he interrogated George on his Darian's bloodline. He spent the afternoon tracing back through the information George possessed. Leaning back in his chair, he carefully thought about his first Darian, Kaf'enir. She had been a beautiful, creamy brown, just like the hot drink they'd called kafinee, which was now called coffee.

He had called her Kafinee, after the drink, not realising how close it was to her real name. And then there had been her foal, Kaf'eder, whom he'd never really had the chance to appreciate. He hoped Warren had bonded with him; Warren deserved to have a Darian. Maybe he would search the archives and see if it was recorded.

Versillion halted on the threshold of the records room, aghast at the sight of his brother in a flood of tears. He strode forward and gathered him in his arms. "Birlerion! Whatever is the matter?"

Birlerion shook in his arms as he tried to control his emotions. "I'm sorry," he gasped. "It was just that George said Pa found Kaf'enir in Vespers. I wanted to know what happened to her."

Versillion tightened his grip. He knew how much Kaf'enir meant to Birlerion. That was why this new Darian was so important. Darians bonded for life, and losing that bond was like losing a piece of yourself that could never be replaced, an empty void forever, or so he had heard.

He bent his head as Birlerion said in a low voice, "Pa bonded with Kaf'enir. I thought he would bond with Kaf'eder, her foal, but no. They kept each other company until he died. Penner bonded with Kaf'eder and struck up a friendship with Tiv'erna, strengthening the bond between Greens and the Atolea. No wonder they kept their word."

"I'm sure it wasn't just that. Janis honoured you as a son of her family, Birlerion. She wouldn't break her word. For Tiv'erna, I'm sure it was a way of keeping your memory alive. They must have missed you."

Birlerion's shoulders shook. "I miss them."

"I do, too," Versillion said, hugging his brother close. He let Birlerion cry until he began to wheeze. "Enough, Birlerion. You'll make yourself ill again, and I intend to beat you in the sparring ring tomorrow."

Birlerion let out a watery chuckle. "That is a given."

"What was is that Pallinten used to say?"

"Skill is more important than strength," Birlerion replied with a grin.

"Exactly. Tomorrow, we'll see how much skill you can remember. Hopefully not a lot."

6

The next morning, Birlerion worked his way through the phases of Apeiron, warming up his muscles and aligning his mind to his body, ready for the thrashing he knew he was about to experience. He had never matched Versillion in the ring; Versillion's strength was many times greater than his. In his youth, if he had come up against someone like Versillion, he would have scarpered.

Still, he needed the training, and Versillion was offering. He could almost match Tagerill after many years of practice, but Versillion would be a workout. He arrived at the sparring ring on time. It wasn't really a ring, more a spare corral that was currently empty, but it would do.

A gleaming chestnut stallion bobbed his head over the railing, his coal-black eyes observing them as they circled. He jerked back at the first clash of steel, but drifted back to watch as the men continued to thrust and parry. He lost interest as the slighter man ended up in the dust again and cantered off to the other side of his field.

Versillion offered his hand to Birlerion. "You nearly had me there," he said with a grin.

"Yeah, right. Nowhere close."

"You were closer than you think. Again."

They continued until Versillion called a stop. "Enough. I know you. You won't stop until you fall over. After lunch, you can give me an archery lesson."

Birlerion cast a glance at him while rubbing his sweaty face with a towel. "You don't need me to teach you."

"You are the best; a free lesson from you is priceless. It's about time I benefited from your skill. I rarely use the bow. I'm not that good at it."

"It's all that muscle. It befuddles your brain."

With a soft snort, Versillion grabbed Birlerion and wrestled him to the ground, releasing him only when he started to choke on the dust. "You're lucky I am considerate of your health, otherwise you'd be eating dirt," Versillion said, rising and pulling Birlerion up with him. He slung his thick arm around his brother's shoulder, and they walked back up to the house, laughing.

The week passed with sparring and archery lessons until, one day, Birlerion paused as he sighted his arrow down the archery range. He hesitated and turned back to Versillion. "Aren't you being derelict in your duty? Shouldn't you be helping Simeon instead of me?"

"Someone has to keep an eye on you," Versillion said as he leaned on his bow.

Birlerion snorted. "I thought that was what Marguerite was doing."

Versillion grinned. "She can't watch you all the time." Jerking his head at the range, he asked, "Why do you think this is here?"

Birlerion shrugged. "Simeon's men need to practice."

"No, because of you. Pa insisted we always have a range so you could practice. Many a time, it's been suggested that this land could be put to better use, but it's never changed; there's always been an archery range at Greens, even though archery isn't so prevalent these days with the new crossbows. Simeon told me that there was a request in the family book to preserve the range, and it's always been honoured."

"But why?"

"Because you personify Greens, Birlerion. Yes, we adopted you, but you brought so much to our family that Pa didn't want to lose."

"What about the rest of you? You were *of* Greens, all here before me, and you all brought your own strengths. Why didn't he remember you?"

"Idiot, of course he did. The dovecote is still out front in memory of Marianille and her love of birds and the ancestor tree still stands, along with the five-mile ride that Tagerill used to run to get rid of his excess energy."

"And for you?"

"I have my sentinal in the homefield. I couldn't ask for more, and Greens is the legacy that Pa and Penner left us all. She is still vibrant and full of life, welcoming us all home."

Birlerion turned back to the range. "As she will be forever," he said as he released his arrow.

At the end of the following week, Marguerite said her farewells and headed back to Elothia and Taurillion, who had already returned to the grand duke's palace, in Retarfu. She hugged Birlerion. "Look after yourself. Remember, you are newly healed, so don't use the waystones for at least three months. Promise me. I don't want you stranded somewhere in between."

"I promise," Birlerion said, and Marguerite held his eyes before nodding. She hugged Versillion and Frenerion. "Make sure he doesn't," she warned.

"I'll keep an eye on him," Versillion promised.

Later that evening, Birlerion stirred restlessly. "It's been over a month since we lost Kino. I need to go and find him."

Versillion eyed him. "Kino?"

"My Darian."

"Lady Marguerite has barely left the building and you want to jaunt off to Terolia?" Simeon asked while slouching in his chair.

They had all breathed a sigh of relief and shucked off their shoes as they'd relaxed with a drink. Marguerite had kept them on their toes, and it was nice to just relax. Birlerion rolled his head and stared at Simeon. "She knows my plans. By leaving, she was signalling that I could manage on my own. I'm not going to keel over anytime soon."

"Thank the Lady for that," Versillion murmured under his breath.

Birlerion grinned. "If I can borrow a horse, I'll go and visit Maraine. If I hang around here, Jerrol will be chasing me, and I'm not going back to Vespers without Kino."

"You can borrow anything you like. You know that, Birlerion," Simeon said, communing with his glass.

Versillion chuckled. "Strike while the iron's hot. You won't find him this mellow again for ages."

"A horse will do, but if my sentinal could stay in the homefield, I would appreciate it."

"That you never have to ask. Greens is your home, and you are always welcome."

"Thank you." Birlerion relaxed and sipped his brandy. A clock ticked in the comfortable silence.

"You know, you wouldn't think three thousand years have passed. It feels just the same," Versillion said, his voice soft.

"I'll take that as a compliment," Simeon replied. "I'm glad."

~

The next morning, Birlerion and George were in the stables, selecting him a horse. George shifted uncomfortably, still embarrassed about losing Birlerion's horse. "I'm right sorry about your Darian."

"It's wasn't your fault, George. It can't be helped."

"Still, he was in our care."

"Well, let's find another who can help me find him."

"This'un will carry you. He's about right for your weight." George led the chestnut stallion forward.

"And Lord Simeon won't miss him?"

"Nah, his lordship rides the grey and Sentinal Versillion rides the bay. Narell could use the exercise."

"He'll get that. How do you think he'll cope with the heat in Terolia? We're approaching the hot season."

"He should be fine. He has a Darian in his bloodline; not enough to make a difference, but he should acclimatise."

"It seems Greens has had its fair share of Darians over the years," Birlerion commented.

"Oh, arr, we've been lucky."

George saddled up the stallion, and Birlerion took him for a canter through the forest. It felt good to be back in the saddle, and as they started back, he ran through all the possible suspects who could have stolen his Darian. He kept snagging on one; the Kirshans. He would have to go into the heartland the hard way and discover why.

The following day, he approached Simeon about borrowing some money. "I'm sorry to ask, but I never got around to setting up an account, and I can't go into Terolia without being prepared."

Simeon waved him off. "I'm sure your credit is good; in fact, Greens probably holds some of it. Your accounts were never closed. I'll get Garrick to look into it for you. We should have done that already for you and Versillion—and

Tagerill and Marianille, come to that. You're all probably quite rich!"

The next surprise came when Versillion insisted that he was going with Birlerion to Terolia. "You can't go on your own, and I'm not leaving you exposed when you're still recovering. Don't argue. You're not fully back to strength. I've spoken to Simeon, and he agrees. Frenerion will be here, and they can call on Marianille if needed. I sent her a message, so she'll know where we'll be."

Birlerion gave in. He would be glad of the company.

They set off for Deepwater early, before the Watch had even woken. Birlerion had agreed with Versillion's suggestion that they stop and see Tagerill and his wife, Miranda. He hadn't seen his brother Tagerill since before his joining with Lady Miranda nearly a year ago, and he hadn't ridden for a couple of months, so there was no point in overdoing it.

They cut across the country, through the tracts of deciduous trees wreathed in early morning mist. The fresh scent was invigorating and typically Greens. By midday, they turned onto the road that bordered the two Watches and led deeper into Deepwater and eventually up to the manor house.

By the time they arrived, Birlerion was glad to hand Narell over to the stable lads and allow Versillion to lug his saddlebags for him. He was feeling quite shaky as he followed Versillion round to the entrance. Versillion buffered him and took Tagerill's effusive greeting, murmuring a warning into his brother's ear that made Tagerill cast Birlerion a startled glance. He moderated his welcome, even if it was heartfelt. Tagerill was a younger version of Versillion, though much louder, and his hair was a brighter, coppery red.

Birlerion hugged Tagerill before bowing over Lady Miranda's hand. He had not had the opportunity to get to know her well, though, if she was Tagerill's choice, he had no qualms accepting her. She was tall and willowy, with long blond hair which curled around her shoulders, and Birlerion could see the likeness to Simeon.

Alyssa, Miranda's daughter, waited with Jennery at the top of the steps. She held her baby son in her arms and beamed at Birlerion as he slowly climbed the steps. Her smile faded as she obviously recognised his exhaustion. "Lea, help him."

Her husband cast her a startled glance but went to greet Birlerion. Tucking an arm in Birlerion's, he escorted him up the steps, and Birlerion leaned on him, frustrated at his weakness.

"Alyssa, it's so good to see you, and this must be Hugh. Congratulations," Birlerion said as they reached the top.

"Welcome, Birlerion. Come in and rest. You can meet our treasure inside." Alyssa pushed her husband in and followed them into the house, intent on getting Birlerion into a chair before he collapsed. She dumped Hugh in his lap, effectively preventing him from moving once he was seated, and went to welcome Versillion.

Tagerill sat next to him. "Where have you been? Last we heard, you were recovering at Oprimere with Marguerite as a nursemaid, you lucky thing. But it's been months."

Birlerion gave Tagerill a resigned smile as he hugged the dark-haired baby in his arms. He inhaled the sweet smell of new life and talcum. "Although Marguerite is a blessing, I would have preferred not to need her," he said.

Tagerill scowled. "We never did get the full story. Jerrol has been tight-lipped about the whole affair."

"That's because there are no words to explain it. It happened. We won. Let's leave it at that."

Tagerill was about to protest when he caught Versillion's eye and desisted. Miranda grasped Tagerill's hand. "You have been in Greenswatch? How is Simeon?"

"He is well, and we were fortunate in his welcome. My sentinal still resides there."

"As he should," Tagerill said.

Birlerion hunched his shoulders and dropped his face to rest on the baby's head. Hugh waved his arm and Birlerion captured his tiny hand and kissed it. "I was lucky. I was struggling with a chest infection, but his healer, Liria, caught it in time."

Versillion leaned forward. "He is still recovering. No matter what he says, he almost died at Oprimere. Only his sentinal brought him back. It has been two months for a reason; he still has a way to go."

"Versillion, please."

"No, Birlerion, we are with family. They should know that we nearly lost you. We are not going to lose you through lack of knowledge."

"But why are you on the road if you are still recuperating?" Miranda asked, frowning at Birlerion.

"Because he doesn't have anyone to tell him not to," Alyssa said. "It's time you settled down, Birlerion. You need someone to look after you."

Versillion grimaced.

"What?" Jennery asked.

"It doesn't matter. It's in the past," Birlerion said, regretting his conversations with Versillion, where he had shared more than he should. But the memories were so clear, and he had thought he was speaking with his father, and he had needed the reassurance that it wasn't his fault, that those who had died in Vespers as he tried to help Leyandrii, didn't die because of him. Taking a deep breath, he asked, "What about you? How is Deepwater recovering?"

"Slowly," Jennery admitted. "We're still plugging the gaps, though peace on the border helps relieve the urgency."

"I'll bet it does."

"What are you doing here? Not that we aren't pleased to see you, of course," Jennery added.

"We just broke our journey here. We are travelling to see Maraine. There's been a slight hiccup with me bonding with my Darian."

"He was stolen over a month ago. Birlerion intends on retrieving him," Versillion said.

Birlerion twisted his lips. "I need to speak with Maraine before I go charging off to retrieve anything. I don't want to make it any worse for her."

Tagerill whistled. "You think the Atoleans stole him?"

"No, not at all, but she might have heard of any discontent. Hopefully, she can narrow down the places to look."

Tagerill stared at him, doubt written all over his face. "Are you sure you are up for this? You can't search the desert; it's huge. Send word to Kayerille. She can scout out for you."

"I intend to ask her, but they'll move him if they get suspicious. I want to be there. I'll know it's him, and once we bond, I'll know where he is. Without that link, we'll find it difficult to prove he is the right horse."

"I'll keep an eye on Birlerion," Versillion said.

Tagerill burst out laughing, and Birlerion hugged Hugh close as he flinched at the sudden noise. "You are going to Terolia with him?"

"Why not?"

"You. In the desert?"

Versillion lowered his eyebrows as he glared at his brother. "I have been to Terolia before, you know. I know what to expect."

"Birlerion, take me. He won't last two minutes."

Birlerion chuckled. "I am quite sure Versillion will be fine, and anyway, you have your hands full here." He shifted Hugh onto his shoulder and patted his back. He caught Alyssa's eye, and she came to retrieve her son.

"He likes you," she murmured. "He hasn't been this quiet in ages."

"He's adorable. You must be so proud."

Jennery said over them, "I'm surprised Simeon can manage without you, Versillion. That only leaves Frenerion, doesn't it?"

"Frenerion will manage. They can always send for Marianille if needs be. Simeon wanted to send a representative. He feels bad about losing the Darian. He thinks it is Greens' fault."

"Tagerill can swing by and keep an eye out whilst you are gone," Jennery suggested. "It won't take much more to sweep the borders as well."

Versillion nodded his thanks. "That would be appreciated."

"But if it's been over a month." Jennery turned back to Birlerion. "The trail will be cold by now."

"I know. That's why I'm not trying to follow it. It would be a waste of time now, especially as there were no sightings reported when Simeon sent out his men. We'll go straight to Mistra and search for the Atoleans from there."

"No sightings at all? I heard he was quite a looker."

"So I'm told. They must have concealed him somehow."

Alyssa returned to the room. "Birlerion, let me show you to your room. You can freshen up before dinner. Lea, you can continue your discussion later. For now, I think Birlerion needs a rest. Yes, you do," she said, overriding Birlerion's protests. "You have time for a nap before dinner." She herded Birlerion out of the parlour and up the stairs.

"Are you sure he should be on the road? Why didn't you use the waystone?" Tagerill asked his brother as Alyssa's determined voice faded.

"Marguerite forbade it for at least three months."

"Three months?" Tagerill was horrified. "You'll be away all year at that rate."

Versillion shrugged. "If that's what it takes. He needs his Darian, Tagerill. I've never seen him so vulnerable and frail; he feels his losses, twice over. It is consuming him and with his injuries I don't think he can take much more. We have to find him."

"What if you don't?" Jennery asked, keeping his voice low.

"Don't even suggest it. We'll find him."

"See?" Alyssa was triumphant as she returned. "He fell asleep straight away. The poor man was exhausted."

"After one day in the saddle?" Tagerill asked with concern.

"He'll improve with time. He is sparring now, and his strength will grow as we travel. If we tried to restrain him in Greens, he would fret even more."

"You were the same, Tagerill. You couldn't wait to get back on a horse. You're all as bad as each other. I'll put dinner back an hour. That should give him enough time to rest." Alyssa vanished, and the conversation turned to the plans for the Watches.

7

A fter a week of travelling, Birlerion squinted at the collection of sandy-coloured buildings, which blended into the desert sands as he and Versillion arrived in the village of Berbera on the Terolian border. They had stopped more often than he thought necessary, but he had given in when his brother insisted. Deep down, he knew his brother had been right, his body ached, and he shifted in his saddle trying to get more comfortable.

The sun was reaching its zenith, and the heat rebounded up from the hard-baked sand as Birlerion led the way into the village and up to the well. He slid from his horse and stared at the empty space where Adilion's tree used to reside.

Versillion pushed past him. He lowered the bucket, hauled it back up, and let the horses drink.

"I forgot his tree wasn't here," Birlerion said, gripping his horse's reins tightly. "It doesn't look right. I understand now what Niallerion meant about there being no sentinal beside the temple."

"It brings it home, doesn't it?" Versillion squinted around the small courtyard. "Funny how something not being there can make such a difference."

"Yeah." Birlerion shook himself. "We'd better speak to the village elder, see if there is any news. Before we leave for Mistra."

"You don't want to stop here tonight?"

"No, let's travel overnight; it will be cooler."

"Won't we get lost in the dark?"

Birlerion chuckled. "No, the stars will guide us. If anything, it's easier."

Versillion shrugged and followed Birlerion deeper into the village. They found the village elder seated in the shade of a building that looked as ancient as he did, held together by baked mud and wishful thinking. Versillion eyed it doubtfully and stood well away from it. The building leaned at a precarious angle, and Birlerion grimaced as he paused before the grey-haired man seated at the entrance. He was sure the building was only standing because it felt like it.

Birlerion clasped his hands in front of his chest in greeting and sank cross-legged before the elder. "Elder, we are travellers from Vespiri, seeking news before we journey onwards."

The elder opened his eyes and stared at him. "My son, the Lady awaits you." He gestured at the weathered building behind him.

Birlerion jerked upright in surprise. "Elder?"

"Don't keep Her waiting any longer," he said and closed his eyes again.

Rising, Birlerion cocked his head at Versillion, who raised his palms and jerked his head at the building. Birlerion grimaced but ducked through the slanted doorway, squinting in the dim light. A single candle burned on the simple altar. He knelt on the sandy floor and waited.

It was peaceful and still. His shoulders relaxed as the scent of roses drifted in the air and he smiled. *"Leyandrii, what are you doing here?"*

"Waiting for you. How are you, Birlerion?"

He heaved a sigh before replying. *"I've been better."*

"Please forgive me for not warning you. My hands were rather full at the time."

"There is nothing to forgive. We did what was necessary."

"I know, but still, Birlerion, know that I am so proud of you; you have exceeded all my expectations."

"Is it over now? Is that the end of the Ascendants?"

"Yes, they will not be returning. I wanted to tell you that this is probably the last time I will be able to visit. The Veil is sealed for good now, and I find it difficult to penetrate its weave. It is very resistant."

Birlerion stiffened. *"But what about the Guardians, the people?"*

"I entrust them to you, Jerrol, and Marguerite. Between the three of you, you should be able to deal with whatever comes next."

"Have you told Jerrol?"

"Yes, though I'm not sure he believed me. He was distracted by the impending birth of his son. You'll have to remind him when the euphoria wears off."

Birlerion chuckled. *"And Marguerite?"*

"She is Remargaren. She will respond, but not necessarily in person. It is difficult to manifest with so little magic in the world. Don't expect to see her often."

"But she's been with me for months."

"Yes, and it wasn't easy for her, but for you, we would do the impossible, just as you do for us. She will sleep unless you call her. Try not to. She is exhausted."

"She never said."

"It would have made no difference. You needed her. Kin'arol is waiting for you. He is in Fuertes. I suggest you follow your plans to enlist Kayerille; you will need her help. And that of the young man encamped to the west. He doesn't know it, but he has been waiting for you. Know that I am pleased. Bless you, Birlerion."

She kissed his forehead, and his exhaustion melted away as a warm flush spread through his body. His uniform shimmered into silver-green desert robes, and a soft breeze caressed his skin as his hand convulsed around an emerald-green headscarf. *"And tell Versillion that my temple will never fall down. I like it just as it is."* Her chuckle faded, and he was alone.

He took a deep breath and exhaled before chanting the Lady's prayer in farewell. He rose and stepped back out into the burning sunshine. Shading his eyes, he grinned at Versillion. "She said you were a coward."

Versillion snorted. "She said no such thing."

Turning to the elder, Birlerion sank to the ground, his robes swirling around him. The elder eyed the shimmering material.

"The Lady is pleased," the elder said.

"Indeed. She mentioned there is someone camped to the west; do you know who it is?"

"Some King's Guards. They don't know what they are doing. The young captain is trying, but his men are stubborn, and they do not listen."

Birlerion's lips twitched. Why was he not surprised? "Are they provisioned sufficiently to journey to Mistra?"

The elder laughed. "They won't make it."

"I see. May I purchase what they need?"

With unexpectedly sinuous grace, the elder rose and led the way behind the temple. He gestured at the tables stacked with goods. "When they are ready, the supplies will be here."

"Thank you. We can start with my brother Versillion. I'll send him in if you would assist him, and I'll take two of the canteens." Birlerion spied poles and canvas. "And enough awnings to protect us all."

The elder's black eyes gleamed. "Of course."

"Good. If necessary, can we store some surplus stuff here until they need it?"

"It would be my pleasure, servant of the Lady."

Birlerion returned to Versillion. "The elder will assist you into the robes. Leave your uniform here until we return."

"How come I didn't get the fancy robes like you?"

"Only the bold are rewarded," Birlerion said with a grin, and he lowered the bucket to fill his canteens.

Once Versillion had been robed appropriately, Birlerion picked up two of the awnings and led the way out of the village and towards the small encampment of tents to the west. The guards were using small two-man tents made of heavier canvas, which would be stifling in this heat. Birlerion shook his head at the sight. His expression grew grimmer as the wilting horses tethered to a rail in the blazing sun came into view.

Dismounting, he ran his hand down the back of the nearest horse. The poor creature's skin was scorching hot, and she blew sadly into the empty bucket at her feet.

"Versillion, help me erect the awnings, quick, before these horses expire, and then go back and get more water." Birlerion offloaded the poles and erected the frame. He whipped the canvas over the top to block the sun but left the front open to catch any breeze that might venture past. He was emptying all his canteens into the buckets for the grateful horses when a sturdy young man peered out of one of the tents and erupted into the sands. "Hey, what do you think you are doing with our horses?"

"Saving them," Birlerion replied, emptying their last canteen and handing it to Versillion. "Go and refill them."

Versillion hesitated as the young man shoved Birlerion's shoulder. "Get away from them. They are not your horses."

"Versillion, please, the horses need the water." Birlerion turned to the youth. "Don't start what you are not prepared to finish, young man. Who is your captain?"

"You're no older than me. Who do you think you are?" The guard swung, and Birlerion side-stepped and then tripped him before pinning him down in the scorching sand. "It is too hot for this foolery. Who is your captain?"

"I am," a familiar voice said from above them, and Birlerion peered up in surprise at the man standing over them.

He released the guard and stood. "Oscar? What are you doing here?"

"Birlerion? I could ask the same of you," replied Oscar Landis, captain of the King's Guard.

The guard stood, watching warily as his captain hugged the strange Terolian.

"Oscar, your horses are not going to last a day in this heat, and nor are you dressed like that."

Oscar grimaced. "I know. Commander Haven was supposed to brief us before we left Deepwater, having reassigned my unit as his Terolian outpost, but he was called away, and it never happened. And then the orders came through, and we had to ship out to Mistra. I've been delaying, hoping for word. I can't tell you how glad I am to see you."

Birlerion blew his breath out. "We're headed that way as well. The Atolea should be camped outside Mistra. We can travel together if you want, but first, let's get out of this heat, and then we'll arrange more appropriate clothing and shelters for your men. They will roast in those tents." More men poked their heads out of their tents; they all looked like broiled lobsters, red-faced and sweating.

The young guard hesitated beside Birlerion and Oscar. "Aren't you hot in all that material?"

Birlerion grinned. "No, the loose robes allow your skin to breathe. Your uniforms are trapping the heat against your skin, which is why you are suffering. There is an elder in the village. He has agreed to supply you all with robes, sandals, and canteens."

"But we'll be court-martialled if we are out of uniform," a stout young man said. His blond hair was plastered to his face and neck.

"No, you won't. Commander Haven would expect you to be dressed appropriately for the terrain you are posted to. In fact, if you are setting up a garrison for him out here, your uniform ought to be adjusted accordingly."

Oscar waved the soldier back to his tent. "Ashton, wait in your tent. Birlerion, introduce me to this elder. Please accompany us to Mistra and whatever you can do to help us would be greatly appreciated."

At that moment, Versillion rode up, festooned with canteens.

Birlerion grinned as his brother dismounted. "Versillion, water Oscar's men for him, would you? Small sips only. Don't let them drink too much too quickly; they look like they are on the verge of heatstroke."

Versillion shook Oscar's hand. "Captain Landis, what are you doing out here?"

"He's been waiting for us," said Birlerion. "Come on, Oscar. You can use Versillion's horse. Let's ease your men's suffering."

The sun was setting by the time the tents had been dismantled and replaced with the lighter awnings. The men had all changed into robes and were lounging more comfortably on the rugs, their complexions easing as their skin cooled. Each had a canteen, which was their new best friend. Oscar, on Birlerion's advice, had threatened dire punishment for any man found without one.

The guards gazed at the Sentinal while he built a fire and started to boil water. He grinned at their shocked expressions as he offered them mugs of coffee. "It's kafinee. You'll be surprised how much a hot drink helps to keep you cool.

That's why the Terolian's drink so much tea. And of course, it's another way of getting fluid into you."

"Kafinee?" Oscar asked, sniffing the drink.

"Sorry, coffee. We used to call it kafinee."

Oscar sipped his drink as he watched the fire. "How come you know so much about the desert, Birlerion?"

Birlerion eased back from the fire and sipped his kafinee. "Experience, I suppose. I was posted to the borders once. Spent a few months out here with Adilion and Kayerille."

The guards perked up, interested. "Was it the same as it is now?" one of them asked.

"Pretty much. The terrain shifts, but the sands are the same, and the heat. Always carry water; your life depends on it. If you ever get caught out in the desert without water, you're dead." He looked around at the attentive men. "I mean it. You check, double-check, and triple-check that your canteen is always full and tied securely to your saddle, preferably you should have two canteens."

"Ok, so we have water and the right clothing. What else do we need?" Oscar asked.

"Always look after your mount. If you are hot, he is probably twice as hot. He's carrying you, after all. When you stop, you always water your horse first and shade him if you can. You cannot walk out of the desert. If you lose your mount, you are dead."

Oscar looked at Birlerion dubiously. "That's a lot of water."

"The pack horses should only be carrying your tents, feed, and water. You carry water and travel rations and anything else you need to survive. You can cook meals when you are in the towns. Out in the desert, what you carry keeps you alive." He looked around at the men. "Tomorrow, you are going to pack up all your extra stuff and leave it here. You carry only what you need to survive, no extraneous baggage. Learn to travel light. An extra canteen of water is better than a book or change of clothes. When you get to Mistra, you can arrange a baggage train to bring you anything else you really need."

"Adilion; he was one of the Sentinals who fell at Oprimere, wasn't he?" a tentative voice asked. It was the young guard who had accosted Birlerion.

"Your name?" Birlerion asked.

"Sergeant Ashton."

"Yes, he was from Berbera. His sentinal used to shade the well. He is on the plateau now with the others." Birlerion's faltered as a myriad of emotions threatened to overwhelm him. He couldn't believe his friends were gone, the loss immediate and painful.

Versillion took up the narrative. "Never travel in the middle of the day. Set up your awnings to protect you and the horses. Wait the heat out, and sleep if you can."

"Doesn't that mean you are out in the heat longer?" Ashton asked. He seemed to be the spokesperson.

"Not really," Birlerion said. "You'll find you don't make much progress in the heat. It just saps all your energy. More efficient to wait it out. If you can travel at night, it's much cooler."

"At night?" the men exclaimed. "How do you know where you are going?"

Birlerion huffed. "Do none of you look up? Sometimes I wonder what the scholars do. They don't seem to have retained anything from the past."

Oscar leaned back and peered up at the sky. "What are we supposed to be looking at?" he asked as he frowned at the sparkling array of stars above them in the clear night sky.

"Seriously?" Birlerion shook his head. "What is the most obvious constant you can see in the night sky?"

"The Lady's moon," Ashton said.

"And where does the Lady's moon rise and set?"

"She rises in the east and sets in the west, same as the sun."

"So, you know where east and west are, then, don't you?"

The men murmured.

"If you stand with your left arm pointed at the rising moon in the east and your right arm in the opposite direction, which way will you be facing?"

"South," a ginger-headed boy with a freckled face said.

"And you are?"

"Private Sanderson, sir."

"Well, Private Sanderson, you are correct, so you now have a compass."

The boy grinned.

"But the moon moves," Ashton complained.

Birlerion chuckled. "But you know where it is moving to. You know she will set in the west. But what else is in the sky?"

There was silence until Oscar said, "Stars."

"Yes, and they make patterns if you look hard enough. For example, see that bright star, the one that glows blue just below the Lady's moon?"

The men squinted at the sky.

"If you move to the right, there is a row of four stars perpendicular to the Lady's moon. It is called the Lady's spear, and it points directly at that red star below it. If you keep the spear in front of you and pointing at the red star, you will be going north."

"But doesn't it move like the moon?" Ashton asked, staring at the sky intently.

"Observe it, and you tell me."

Oscar grinned at the upturned faces. "Birlerion, I can't thank you enough."

"We've hardly scratched the surface. There are many

more constellations that can help with navigation. But they are enough to start with." Birlerion stood and stretched as the watch changed. The newcomers were inundated with instructions on how to navigate using the night sky. "I'm going to get some sleep. We need to start early if we want to reach Mistra before nightfall. Lady bless you, Oscar."

"Lady's blessing. Sleep well, Birlerion."

The next morning, Birlerion was ruthless. He swept through the guards' belongings and forced them to bag everything up and leave it with the elder. By sunrise, Birlerion and Versillion had checked their water canteens. They were mounted, only carrying their weapons, the canteens, and a bare minimum of food. Oscar held his horse as he stood beside Birlerion. "I've never travelled so light," he murmured.

"Believe me, you'll be wishing you didn't have to carry your weapons by the time we reach Mistra." Birlerion twisted in his saddle and raised his voice. "No speaking. An open mouth uses up moisture. Keep an eye on your partner. If anyone looks like they might fall out of the saddle, shout. When we stop, water your horses first, then yourselves, and then erect the awnings."

Oscar rotated his arm, and the column moved out. Birlerion squinted at the sun and pulled his green scarf across his face. Oscar copied him. They'd left later than Birlerion would have liked, but they were still earlier than they could have been, so he led the way into the golden sands. The guards trailed after him, with Versillion bringing up the rear.

Birlerion rode up and down the column, checking the men and encouraging some to drink water. They were perspiring heavily even under the robes. It would take them time to acclimatise.

As the sun reached its highest point, he called a stop, and

the men watered the horses, before taking gulps themselves, and then they began to erect the awnings. Birlerion offered the men a small hessian bag full of salt, that the elder had pressed on him. "Take a pinch. As you perspire, you lose salt," Birlerion said repeatedly, much to the guards' disgust. "Rest. Sleep if you can."

He made sure each of the watch guards had a full canteen. "Small sips, little and often, and change guards every hour."

He joined Oscar in his awning, where he loosened his robes and lay down, groaning as he curled on his side.

"Are you alright, Birlerion?" Oscar murmured, half asleep.

"Yeah, this heat is a killer," Birlerion said as he dozed off.

Versillion woke him after two hours, and they swapped places. Birlerion wrapped himself back up in his scarves as he took up the watch. He gazed out across the golden sands. It was scorching, and sweat trickled down his back as he squinted across the dunes. He was eager to keep moving, but he knew the men needed a break from the glaring sun. Its rays beat down on him, and his tense muscles relaxed as he adjusted to the rhythm of the desert. He had always liked Terolia and its people; in a way, it felt like coming home.

Two hours later, he roused the sluggish guards; most had managed to get some sleep. He made them all drink and then top off their canteens from their stock, careful not to spill any before they remounted.

They trailed into Mistra the following evening, having taken two days to travel what normally took a day. The sun was setting as they wound their way through the city streets, watched by the suspicious townsfolk. Oscar frowned. "We're supposed to meet Sentinal Kayerille in the central square, and she will introduce us to the city officials."

"If she knew you were arriving today, she might meet

you, but I doubt she got the message." Birlerion pulled up in the shade of a spindly tree next to a communal well. "Stop here and water your horses. I'll go and find Kayerille." He grinned at Versillion. "Try and stay out of trouble until I get back."

Versillion scowled at him. "Back at you."

Birlerion continued to chuckle as he rode down a side street, heading towards the older part of the city. His laughter died as he weaved through narrow alleys and older buildings. Finally, he reached a wider street, where a tall sentinal tree stood next to a small domed temple. A grey stone fountain stood before it, once adorned by a statue of the Lady but now weathered to an unrecognisable lump.

He dismounted and lay a hand against the smooth silver trunk. It warmed beneath his palm, and he called Kayerille, hoping she would be home. Otherwise, he would have to traipse all over the city looking for her. The pointy leaves rustled in welcome as Kayerille shimmered out of her sentinal.

"Birlerion," she gasped as she hugged him with delight. "What are you doing here?"

"Escorting your new garrison of King's Guards to Mistra," he replied with a grin.

"What?" Her smooth complexion wrinkled as she frowned at him.

"Jerrol sent Oscar Landis and his men out here to set up the Terolian outpost."

She stared at him blankly. "An outpost? To do what?"

Birlerion stared back at her. "Do you mean to tell me you know nothing about this?"

"No, I've heard nothing from the Captain since Oprimere."

"Ascendants' balls! Wait until I get hold of him. Not only did he send Oscar out here completely unprepared, but he has no base to set up in. He has sixteen men without a clue how to survive in the desert. Kayerille, you are going to have your work cut out for you."

"Me? Why me?"

Birlerion grinned at the young woman before him. Exquisite, coffee-coloured skin covered a lithe body that was primed for action. Her lustrous black hair was drawn off her face in a neat plait, and her silver eyes were even more startling against her dark complexion. A wicked scimitar hung from her belt, and he knew she had daggers strapped to her thighs beneath the amber-coloured robes she wore.

"Because you are the incumbent Sentinal, you get to host them. And introduce them to the city officials. And make sure they stay alive."

"Birlerion, you can't just dump seventeen greenhorns on me."

"Why not?"

"Because I have no idea what to do with them."

"Teach them to survive and how to fight in the desert, of course."

"With what?"

"Why, the skills you were born with, of course."

Kayerille slapped his arm.

"Don't worry. Versillion is here with me. We'll help."

"You'd better. Where are they?"

"I left them watering their horses at the central well," Birlerion said, his eyes gleaming.

Kayerille gasped. "You did what?"

"Where else was I going to leave them?"

She muttered under her breath as she stalked down the street. Birlerion led his horse and followed. She stopped, aghast at the congestion she found in the central square.

"Where would you recommend I billet them?" Birlerion murmured from behind her.

She whipped around, and as she met his amused eyes, she scowled at him. "You just wait." She strode into the confusion and unerringly found Landis. "Captain Landis, you can't stay here."

Landis ran a hand through his black hair, his thin face looking harried. "Sentinal Kayerille, thank goodness. I don't know where we're supposed to go, and more people keep turning up to stare at us. Where's Birlerion?"

"Here," Birlerion said with an unrepentant grin.

"We're the latest attraction."

"I'm sure it's your blue eyes. They are so unusual here in Terolia. Most of them won't have seen them before."

"Birlerion." Kayerille whacked him again. "You are not being helpful."

Birlerion grinned.

Kayerille rolled her eyes. "Landis, there's an empty administrator's building off the western marketplace. It has stables and plenty of room. We need to get your men off the streets. You can stay there until we sort this mess out. Follow me."

She hurried down a side street, and Oscar corralled his men and followed her. Versillion joined Birlerion at the tail of the column. "What is so amusing?"

"Jerrol forgot to tell Kayerille that Oscar was coming to Mistra to set up the King's Terolian Guards."

"Oh," Versillion said. "Oh," he repeated, his eyes widening. "That could be awkward."

"Indeed."

"It's not funny."

"Sure, it is. I can't wait to see how Kayerille and Oscar manage it."

Versillion cocked an eyebrow at him. "How they manage it?"

"It's not our problem. We are searching for my horse, not setting up a new barracks."

"Somehow, I don't think they will see it that way."

Birlerion burst out laughing. "That's what makes it so amusing."

Versillion shook his head, though his lips did start to twitch as he imagined Kayerille's response.

8

L andis breathed a sigh of relief as his men returned to some semblance of normality. The familiar routine of stabling and caring for their horses superseded the need to survive under the blazing hot sun. The administration building turned out to be a collection of flat roofed buildings built around a central open courtyard. Red clay formed the outer walls, and the inner walls were alleviated by small open windows with slatted shutters, which made the chambers very dark. The central courtyard was large enough for a sparring ring and gave access to the stables, which ran along the east wall.

Landis split his men into three units, one guarding the entrances, one up on the roof, and the others off duty. Once they were organised, he sat and made a list of his priorities. Assuming this would be his base, he needed some support staff.

His thoughts drifted to the stunning Mistran Sentinal. He hoped Kayerille would be able to recommend some help. First on his list was the need to speak with the Mistra officials to straighten out any misapprehensions on what their purpose was. He rubbed his temple. He could already tell this was not going to be straightforward.

He reread his orders and scowled at the unoffending paper.

"They won't change no matter how hard you stare at them," Birlerion said from the doorway.

Landis continued to scowl. "Are you going to help or are you just going to poke fun?"

"But Oscar, think how you can wind Jerrol up about this. He has failed you miserably, and all because he is going to be a father."

"That attitude does not help me."

Birlerion chuckled. "But I'm not officially here. I am still recuperating from my terrible injuries and on a personal venture."

"You *are* here, and you know Terolia. That's good enough for me."

"But think how much fun you will have working with Kayerille. You don't need me in the way."

"Of course I do. You know the families; I need introductions."

"Kayerille can provide those."

"Birlerion, please." Oscar was almost begging.

"You'll owe me."

"Anything."

"I could use some support when I travel inland. It will be a good practice sortie for some of your men."

"Deal, but only once the garrison is secure."

Birlerion grinned at him. "And who makes that decision? I can only stay a couple of weeks. I need to travel up to Fuertes, and that will take at least two weeks. Someone stole my Darian. I don't mind lulling those thieves into a false sense of security, but any longer will be going too far."

"I'll take the two weeks," Oscar said, exhaling with relief.

Kayerille tapped him on the shoulder, and Birlerion stepped into the room. "What thieves?" she asked. "And why can't you use a waystone?"

"Before I left Oprimere, someone stole my Darian from Greens. I've had a chest infection, so Marguerite won't let me use the waystones for a while."

"Oh, no, Birlerion. Do you know where your Darian is?"

"Somewhere in Fuertes. I need to speak to Maraine before I go up there to get him back. Oscar, I have a feeling you are going to have some trouble with the Kirshans. They were noticeably upset by the removal of their Medera."

Kayerille pursed her lips. "And if you have to go by horse, you'll have to go straight through their territory."

Birlerion grimaced. "Any word on where Maraine is encamped?"

"Marmera, last I heard. At least that is on the way to Fuertes."

"Right. First, let's get Oscar sorted. Oscar, show Kayerille your orders; at least she'll have an idea of what you need."

"They are not particularly helpful. Jerrol left them vague as he wasn't sure what we would find." Oscar handed the papers to Kayerille. She skimmed them and frowned.

"Vague isn't the word. Are you supposed to be invading, protecting, or exploring?"

Oscar laughed. "All of the above. We are the king's presence in Terolia, all seventeen of us. I think he needs a toehold just to show he is paying attention."

"Oh, I think you could be more that," Birlerion said. "If we can show you to be the glue holding our two kingdoms together, you could make a huge difference. You need a checkpoint at Berbera to stop those idiots from travelling into the desert unprepared." He waved a hand as Oscar winced. "I don't mean you. At least you had the sense to wait. The

Terolians get distressed by unnecessary bodies cluttering up their deserts."

"Even though I didn't know what I was waiting for," Oscar muttered under his breath.

"The Lady protects," Birlerion said with a grin, "as do I on occasion."

"You're going to help us?" said Kayerille. "Thank goodness. You can start with Elder Var'ena. She needs to approve the reallocation of this building."

Birlerion observed the dank walls. "Are you sure this is the best place for him to set up? This is right in the middle of Mistra. Isn't there anything closer to you in the older quarter?"

"The more central, the better; his men will be immersed in the culture. They need to learn what is normal and what is out of character. They need to learn how to blend in and when to stand out. They have a lot to learn if they are going to be successful here."

"I need some support staff," said Oscar. "We can look after ourselves for a while, but at some point, I'll need infrastructure behind me. Local folk we can trust."

Kayerille pushed Birlerion towards the door. "Let Birlerion negotiate the lease for this place. Then we'll fill it with people."

"Why me?" Birlerion protested. "Oscar, what's your budget?" he called over his shoulder.

"I haven't got one!" Oscar yelled back.

"What?"

"We're supposed to be self-sufficient."

"You mean Jerrol sent you out here with no funds? Why, that copper-pinching …" Birlerion's voice faded as Kayerille dragged him down the corridor.

Three chimes later, a procession of Terolians leading

heavily laden mules entered the stable yard of the newly acquired garrison of the King's Terolian Guard.

The eldest man drew to a halt. "Commander Landis?"

"The captain is in his office. I'll get him for you." Ashton hurried into the dank room that Oscar had chosen for himself after a quick exploration of the ground floor. Landis followed him out into the courtyard and stared at the Terolians, somewhat bemused.

The elderly man bowed, his hands clasped in front of his brown-robed chest. Oscar awkwardly returned the greeting. "Lady's greeting, Commander. I am Dar'ille of the Kiker. I bring the staff and supplies that Elder Var'ena agreed to provide."

"Supplies?" Oscar asked, observing the tattoo on the man's right cheek: a yellow crescent moon, the sign of the Atolea.

"Yes, I am your steward. The elder has assigned us—" the man waved his hand at his colleagues "—to assist you in setting up your … your garrison in the name of King Benedict and Terolia. We welcome you to Mistra and hope your stay will be comfortable."

"Thank you," Oscar replied, not knowing what else to say.

"I apologise for the lack of facilities, but we will soon have the kitchens provisioned and the well reopened. This building has not been used for many years and will require some work to restore its previous comfort." Dar'ille gave Oscar a self-satisfied smile. "It will be our honour to prepare it for you."

"Carry on, then," Oscar said, slightly stunned.

Dar'ille turned and ordered his staff about. They scattered, leading their mules to various parts of the building, clearly familiar with the layout. Oscar retreated to his office, but the sound of banging soon had him peering back out his door. Boards were being removed from the windows, and his office was flooded with light. He sat back down in his chair and grinned as the garrison came to life around him.

Much later, Birlerion and Kayerille returned. They entered laughing, arm in arm, but they stopped and stared at the torchlit courtyard. Ashton saluted them. "Sentinals, welcome to the garrison of the King's Terolian Guards," he chanted, a huge grin on his face.

Birlerion's jaw dropped. "Well, Elder Var'ena wasn't joking."

Kayerille punched his shoulder. "See, I said you were the best man for the job."

Landis, standing in the doorway, beckoned them over, and then he ushered them into his newly cleaned office and shut the door. "Birlerion, how much is this going to cost me? Don't get me wrong, it's amazing, but I told you, I don't have any budget."

Birlerion grinned. "You could have said no."

"You try stopping them. They are following the elder's orders, and nothing will stop them."

"Tell him," Kayerille said, a smile on her face.

"The Mistran Elders are honoured that King Benedict of all of Vespiri and Terolia chose their city to host the first garrison of the Terolian guards. It is their duty to provide the guards with all they need to fulfil their duties. The Lady blesses them, and they thank the Lady."

Oscar stared at him.

Birlerion's lips twitched. "As such, the Elders offer a monthly tithe of people and vittles to sustain their king's representative. They beg that, should there be anything they overlooked, the Commander of the Terolian Guards—that's you, by the way—should not hesitate to speak up, and they will do their utmost to fulfil his needs."

Oscar worked his way through it all. "And what do they expect in return?" he asked with suspicion.

Birlerion couldn't help it. A burst of laughter escaped him, and he folded over, holding on to Kayerille. "Your face!" he said as he got his laughter under control. Oscar's scowl deepened, and Birlerion giggled again. "Sorry, but you should see your face." He cleared his throat and made an effort to compose himself. "Um, oh, yes, in return, the garrison of the Terolian guards will protect the Terolian people from all threats in the name of the king." He glanced at Kayerille and muttered out of the side of his mouth, "Was that all of it?"

"You forgot the representation bit."

"Oh yes, the Commander of the Terolian Guards is expected to sit on the Mistran council meetings to represent the king. I thought that might be useful."

"Useful?" Oscar's breath exploded out of him.

Birlerion peered at him. "Don't you think so?"

Oscar gaped at him like a stranded fish.

"Does that mean he's pleased?" Kayerille asked. "You know him better than me."

"I think he is overwhelmed with gratitude at all our excellent work and doesn't know how to thank us," Birlerion replied with a grin.

"Birlerion!" Oscar got his voice under control. "How did you do it?"

"A lot of fast-talking, and now I need a drink, a strong one. Kayerille, lead me to a bar. I need fortification before Oscar gives me another task."

"If you are getting a drink, then you can buy me one, too," Oscar said, following them out of his office.

"I think you ought to buy me one," Birlerion complained. He stared around the brightly lit courtyard. "Where is Versillion?"

"He was sparring earlier, or at least that's what he called it. I'm not sure those brave enough to get in the ring agreed."

Birlerion let out another belt of laughter, and Oscar glared at him. "Why are you so happy?"

"I'm not sure. The Lady blesses us, and we bathe in her glory. I feel really good. Long may it continue."

Oscar grinned. "Then let us celebrate our good fortune and your happiness. I wouldn't want to miss out on either."

Kayerille took them to a local bar, introduced them to the owner, and sat back as Birlerion proceeded to befriend everyone and drink them all under the table.

By the end of the night, only Birlerion was still standing, singing the Lady's hymn under his breath. Versillion found him staring up at the moon, hugging a wine bottle.

"Birlerion?"

Birlerion lurched round and peered at his brother. "Versssilll?"

Versillion grabbed Birlerion's arm and forced him into a chair. Looking around, he saw Landis and Kayerille slumped against each other over a table. "What have you done?"

"We're sssellerbrating."

Versillion went to find the owner and ordered plenty of black coffee. He forced Birlerion to take a mug as he tried to wake Oscar up. "Oscar, drink the coffee. You can't let your men see you like this, nor the elders; not on your first night."

Oscar groaned but took the mug. "My head," he said, looking around blearily. "Where are we?"

"In a bar, you fool. What were you thinking?"

"Birlerion was happy. We wanted to make the most of it."

Versillion stared at Birlerion before crouching in front of him. "Birlerion? What is it?"

Birlerion tilted his head and drank his coffee, keeping his silver eyes on his brother. "Why does it have to be anything?"

"You never get drunk."

"'Bout time I did, then. Can't go through life never getting drunk."

Kayerille stirred as Oscar nudged her. He shoved a mug under her nose, and she inhaled and opened her eyes.

"What happened?" Versillion asked.

"Nothing," replied Birlerion.

"It's not nothing."

"Versillion." Birlerion sighed. "Leave it."

"What did Leyandrii say?"

Kayerille looked up, her eyes widening.

"She said goodbye." Birlerion's eyes shone with unshed tears.

Versillion gripped his shoulder. "You fool. It's not forever. She will return."

Birlerion's lips twisted. "You think? She said goodbye, Versillion," he whispered. "She said she could no longer cross the Veil, and she was leaving Remargaren in our hands. Mine, Jerrol's and Marguerite's. She left me her blessing."

Exhaling, Versillion hugged him. No wonder Birlerion had been drinking. Exulting in the Lady's blessing whilst grieving for her and his lost friends. Such a contradiction of emotions would make anyone resort to drink. "Come on. Let's get you all back to the barracks. You'll be glad to know you have a bed made up. Whether you'll be able to get out of it tomorrow is another thing, but you deserve to have a headache."

Oscar scowled at them. "I'm never going out with you again, Birlerion. I thought you were the sensible one."

Birlerion's laugh was hollow. "Not me. Find an impossible task and send for Birlerion. He'll deal with it. And if he's lucky, he might be one of the ones to live and tell the tale." He closed his eyes.

Versillion watched him. "No going to sleep here. Kayerille, get his other arm. Oscar, don't you dare stagger."

Versillion herded them back to the garrison. The sentries averted their eyes, though they grinned as their commander overcorrected as he passed through the gates.

Kayerille and Birlerion collapsed in a muddle on his bedroll, and Versillion shrugged and left them there. At least they were on a bed. Oscar managed to find his room and wallowed in his bed until the blinding sun woke him in the early hours of the next morning.

He groaned as his head thumped. A jug of water sat next to him, and he blessed Versillion and drank the lot before shedding his clothes, washing, and finding a clean robe. He went off to find a bucket so he could shave, but when he came to it, his hand trembled so much he thought better of it and retreated to his office.

A sachet of powder and a glass of water sat on his desk, and he fell on them with relief, wondering who had left him the painkiller. He looked up as Versillion hovered in the doorway.

"How's the head?" Versillion asked.

"Don't ask. Thanks for the powder."

"Birlerion has a stash, though that's something you ought to ask the elders about; access to a healer. Your men are more liable to get injured out here."

"Good point. How is he this morning?"

"Subdued."

"So, he's awake?"

"Oh, yes. He's been doing Apeiron for hours."

"What was yesterday all about?"

"I'm not sure. Birlerion rarely drinks, certainly not that much. I wonder if he was saying goodbye. He hasn't had the chance to grieve like the rest of us. Those we lost were all good friends of his, and if the Lady did say goodbye, then that might have tipped him over the edge. He won't talk about it, and once he gets tight-lipped, you may as well forget it."

"The Lady said goodbye?"

"That's what he said last night, though he wasn't too sober."

Oscar grimaced. "None of us were. At least I know to steer clear of the local wine. How is Kayerille?"

"At about the same stage as you."

Oscar chuckled and then groaned, holding his head. "I'll never drink with him again."

"Don't say that. You all had such fun."

"Yeah, right, and what's the price for fun?"

"A delegation from the Elder Council to say hello."

Oscar stiffened. "What?"

"I came to warn you that they are on their way."

"Lady help us. I haven't even shaved."

"Never mind. Just say you are growing a beard to blend in."

Oscar glared at him. "Go and get Birlerion. He got us into this; he can suffer with me."

Versillion smiled sadly. "I would say he has suffered enough already, but here he comes. He must have heard you." He moved out of the doorway to let his heavy-eyed brother in.

"Forgive me, Oscar. I'm not sure what came over me last night," Birlerion said as he halted on the threshold.

"I could have said no." Oscar grimaced. "It's not your fault. But we have more important matters. A delegation is arriving. Could you do the introductions? I wish I had time to shave, but I'm afraid I'll cut my throat."

Birlerion looked him over. "You look fine. They won't notice. Just don't throw up on their feet."

"Thank you for that enlightening advice."

Birlerion's grin was a shadow of the previous evening's, and Oscar wondered if he would ever see Birlerion so carefree again.

9

The brand new Terolian King's Guards snapped to attention as the Terolian delegation entered the garrison. Birlerion met them in the courtyard and led them over to Oscar. He gestured to the mature woman dressed in yellow robes and draped in colourful scarves. "Elder Var'ena, may I introduce Commander Landis."

Oscar bowed with his hands clasped against his chest. He rose and met her hard black eyes. "Elder, may I say thank you for your kind welcome and support. I'd show you around, but I expect you are more familiar with this building than I am, and your people are still opening it up."

"Commander, they are your people now. I hope they have been satisfactory?"

"Oh, yes. The king will be most pleased."

"Good. Jar'alla here will be your liaison. He will advise you of the dates of our meetings and other news of import." Oscar acknowledged the bow of a shorter young man attired in brown robes. The third man also wore brown robes, but he was much thinner and his shoulders were bowed as if he carried a heavy weight. His expression was supercilious, and he was bare-cheeked, so he had no obvious affiliation. He glared at Oscar. Var'ena's eyes glittered as she introduced him. "Rin'urda is responsible for safety on the streets of Mistra. He will report to you. We will leave him with you so he can inform you of his current processes."

"Elder, I am not only responsible for Mistra. I will need to liaise with the other cities as well."

The elder waved her hand. "Of course, but a commander of your stature will manage. After all, you have three Sentinals in your retinue," she said as if that explained everything. "I also sent a message to Medera Maraine requesting her presence. I understand you want to speak with her."

Oscar paled. "I would not wish to inconvenience the Medera."

"Nonsense. She is the closest Medera. You ought to inform her of your requirements. Her people will need to work with you." The elder nodded and, on that final comment, led her companions back out of the garrison.

Oscar exhaled slowly and looked at Rin'urda. "Please, join me in my office." He glanced over at Birlerion. "I expect to see you straight after."

Birlerion bowed. "Of course, commander."

Oscar observed the slight man seated opposite him. He was perched on the edge of his chair as if he didn't intend on staying very long. It was very clear the man didn't want to be there, and no doubt, he resented being told that he had to report to Oscar. Well, he would have to learn fast if he wanted to keep his position.

"Tell me about yourself, Rin'urda. Where do you hail from, and how long have you held this post?" asked Oscar.

"I've lived in Mistra all my life."

"You haven't been to any of the other towns?"

"No, there is no point. I am only responsible for Mistra."

"We'll have to get you out and about. We will need to liaise with the other councils."

"I'm not interested in travelling. I'm not a nomad; I prefer the city."

"Doesn't that limit your contacts and your understanding of the issues currently affecting your city?"

"I know all that needs to be known about Mistra." Rin'urda looked down his nose at Oscar, a self-satisfied smile hovering over his mouth.

"Oh? Then tell me."

Rin'urda stared at him. "What?"

"Tell me what is happening in your city. What I need to be made aware of."

"Nothing." Rin'urda raised his chin.

"What do you mean, nothing?"

"There's nothing you need concern yourself with."

"There is nothing of interest or you know nothing?"

"Nothing of interest."

Oscar leaned forward and rested his elbows on his desk. "Let me make myself clear. If you cannot provide me with the information I require, then you are of no use to me, and I will find someone who can."

Rin'urda held Oscar's gaze for all of a minute, and then he deflated. "Yes, sir."

"Good. Which family are you affiliated with, Rin'urda?"

"I'm not, sir."

Oscar smiled grimly. "You are now. You are part of my family, that of the Terolian guards. Your allegiance is to me and my men. If I find out you have betrayed any of us, your punishment will be as if you betrayed your family according to Family Law. Do I make myself clear?"

"Y-yes, sir," Rin'urda stuttered, shrinking in his chair.

"Can I trust you, Rin'urda?"

"Yes, sir."

"I hope so, for your sake. Now, let's try again. What do I need to know about the city of Mistra?"

Rin'urda started talking.

Finally, Oscar called the meeting to an end. "I think that is enough for now. I get the gist. Where do you live?"

"Near the council offices, sir."

"Well, I think we'll move you here. I need an assistant, and I think you will fit the bill, and you need to get to know my men. You can keep your office at the council, but you'll split your time equally between here and there."

"Yes, sir."

Oscar grinned at the man. Without his arrogant sneer, he had shed years. "Don't look so horrified. I think you'll find life will be much more interesting around the garrison. We have much to do for all of Terolia, not just Mistra."

"Yes, sir."

"This Family Law, is it written down anywhere?"

"Yes, sir."

"Bring a copy with you tomorrow. Ninth chime sharp. I expect you to have moved in by then. Your office will be next door. I'll leave you to arrange it how you want."

"Yes, sir."

A chime later, Birlerion leaned against his office doorframe. "You should get out in the sparring ring, Oscar. Help relieve some of that tension."

"Are you offering?"

"In my weakened state? I would be a pushover. Maybe try Kayerille or Versillion. After all, we are all at your command."

"Birlerion! What did you tell the elders, for Lady's sake?"

Birlerion shrugged himself off the door and sat in the chair. "Only that you are the king's representative and in command of all things to do with security in Terolia."

"I can't run around after every petty thief!"

"Of course not. That's why it was important to get the local forces reporting to you. They will be responsible for keeping the peace here in Mistra and you'll have access to their men. You should do the same with the Sentinals and guards in the other cities. It won't make much difference to them, as they will be pretty autonomous, but it will *look* like you are in overall command."

"So, I'm going to have to travel all over this desert?"

"Afraid so, but think of your network. The Sentinals can use waystones and get you intelligence so much faster, and they will feel more connected. I suggest you ask Kayerille to teach you how to survive and fight Terolian style. You will need it, as will your men."

Oscar held his head in his hands. "What are you trying to do to me? And the Medera as well? She is going to string me up."

"No, she won't. I am here."

"You know, I never thought of you as big-headed, but I'm beginning to wonder. Why will your presence make a difference?"

"Tsk, tsk, Oscar. Don't you remember? I am a son of the Atolea. I am family."

Resting his chin on his hand, Oscar stared at him. "So? The elder said *I* wanted to speak to the Medera, not you."

Birlerion grimaced. "Once she sees me, the fact that you requested her presence will go out of her head. The Atolean honour has been brought into question. They have lost my Darian."

"About that; why would anyone steal your horse?"

"I don't know, but I think the contract between Greens and the Atolea has become public. It is possible that someone was looking for a way to challenge them. As the Atolea have risen, so the Kirshans have fallen. Maybe someone wanted to even the scales."

"It sounds a bit convoluted for Terolians."

"Don't underestimate them. They may be nomads at heart, but their lives are controlled by law and regulations. They abide by Family Law or pay the price. You need to learn it; you will no doubt be dragged in to mediate. You need to know what drives them."

"Something else to add to my list."

"I'd put it at the top," Birlerion advised, his face serious as he rose. "I'll be watching your men in the sparring ring if you change your mind."

Oscar pushed his way through the circle of men and halted at the edge of the ring. Birlerion was stripped to the waist, his pale skin gleaming with sweat as he and Kayerille, who was dressed only in vest and trousers, clashed swords. They were both barefoot and using curved scimitars, which flashed in the sun. Oscar's men hissed in astonishment at the swirling dance Birlerion and Kayerille performed.

Versillion joined Oscar, his frown deepening as he watched. He stepped forward. "Break!" he shouted, and Birlerion and Kayerille spun to a standstill, chests heaving. "What do you think you are doing? Birlerion, you are only half-fit. Are you mad?"

Kayerille gasped. "What?"

"Don't any of you listen? He was left for dead at Oprimere. He is only just out of his sickbed, for Lady's sake." Versillion's anger was palpable.

"Well, if he fights like that now, there is no way I'm getting in a ring with him when he's fit," Sanderson said, and the men murmured agreement around him.

Kayerille was horrified. "Birlerion, why didn't you say? If you had faltered, I could have killed you."

"I needed to spar properly. It felt good," Birlerion replied, wheezing.

"Well, no more. Go clean up. You are on bed rest until further notice, and that's an order," Versillion snapped.

Birlerion grimaced but handed his sword to Ashton. As he turned, he stumbled, and Versillion grabbed his arm and escorted him from the sparring ring.

Kayerille straightened and pointed her sword at Ashton. "You're next."

"You won't fight like that, will you?" he asked as he stepped up.

Kayerille laughed, tossing her plait over her shoulder. "You don't think you can keep up?"

"I don't even know how to use this kind of sword. It even feels different in the hand."

"That's the balance. Your straight swords have the weight at the hilt. These curved swords widen at the end; it changes how they flow. Look." She demonstrated. "See how the sword moves? Curved swords are designed to slash and cut, much better for use from horseback. Your straight swords are better for thrusting. Each has its own benefits. Here in Terolia, you will be facing curved swords, so you need to either learn to use one or how to use your straight sword against it."

Oscar said, "Pair off, one with a curved sword and one with a straight. Who knows when you might need it? We are in Terolia now, men. You were chosen because you were open to learning a new culture. Sentinal Kayerille is willing to teach you. Your education starts now." He nodded at Kayerille and returned to his office.

~

Versillion escorted Birlerion to the shower and then to his room. Birlerion flicked a glance at him. "You don't need to hound me. I will rest."

"I know you will, because I am making sure. If I leave you, you'll do something stupid again."

Birlerion sighed and lay down. "It did feel good," he murmured as he closed his eyes.

Versillion watched him relax until his breathing deepened. Birlerion's face was pale, though fine creases framed his eyes where he had been squinting at the sun. His dark lashes accentuated the paleness. If you looked closely, it was obvious he was not in full health. He was still gaunt beneath the stubble covering his chin. It was only his lean strength that had fooled everyone.

He wheezed as he slept, and Versillion's face tightened with concern. He looked up as Kayerille paused in the doorway. As she peered at Birlerion, she heard the wheeze. "I didn't realise," she said softly. "I would never have sparred with him if I had known how ill he was."

"He's good at hiding it."

"Still, you would never have known from his performance. Why is he here if he's still convalescing?"

"He wants his Darian."

"Oh," Kayerille said, and then, after a small pause, she added, "Then we'd better help find him."

"Indeed," Versillion said.

10

The next day, no one would let Birlerion do anything. Versillion ignored his protests. "One day won't hurt you. And don't try, because the men have orders to stop you. If you behave today, you can do Apeiron tomorrow. That slow exercise will be good for you."

"What am I supposed to do?"

"Nothing. Read a book. Relax. I'll escort you to the temple but nowhere else."

"I don't need an escort."

"Yes, you do."

Birlerion gritted his teeth, but Versillion was unmovable. Maybe he had overdone it, but still, he wouldn't shatter from a bit of exercise. He grumbled but sat in the shade and checked over his weapons, repairing his arrows, tidying up the feathers, and waxing the shafts; busy work just to keep his hands moving.

He observed Oscar's new assistant move into his office. The man seemed well organised and had his new office set up within a few chimes. Every so often, someone passed by, making sure Birlerion was still there. The whole garrison seemed to be rotating around him, and Birlerion wasn't too surprised when, in turn, Rin'urda stopped beside him.

Birlerion squinted up at him. "Come to check up on me?"

Rin'urda squirmed. "They are all worried about you."

"No need. I'll be fine."

"They told me you'd say that. Is it true that someone stole your Darian?"

"Yes, unfortunately."

"And you don't know who?"

"No. He was stolen from a stable in Greens. They caused a fire as a distraction. No one saw them, and there were no sightings of him on the roads."

Rin'urda squatted on the steps. "Determined people always manage to find a way."

Birlerion's hands stilled, and he stared at the arrows in his lap. "Yes," he said, his eyes distant.

Shifting awkwardly, Rin'urda said, "There are only two entry points from Vespiri, really, Ramila or Berbera. They would need to resupply before they could venture further inland."

"It's been over a month since he was stolen. He could be anywhere. Though I believe they are heading for Fuertes."

Rin'urda looked up, startled. "How would you know that?"

"I have it on good authority." Birlerion pressed his lips together. You couldn't get any better authority than Leyandrii's. His heart constricted at the thought of never seeing her again.

Rin'urda frowned. "You think they are trying to hide him in the herds?"

"Why they think that would work is beyond me, especially as he is a Darian and can bespeak others, he could tell another Darian what has happened to him, but that is what I'm told."

"They would have to go via Marmera to get around the ridge. We may find word of them there."

"I'll ask Kayerille to go and speak to Virenion; he is based in Marmera. He may be able to find out something for us," Birlerion said, frowning. He grinned at the young man. "Good idea."

"You Sentinals could be handier than I thought," Rin'urda replied, frowning in turn. "The commander is right. We've become too insular. I had never considered it before …" His voice trailed off as he turned over the new idea.

Birlerion grinned. "Maybe you should suggest a messenger service. Sentinals can provide you with the network, get your people reporting to them, and they can bring you the information in batches. Save you travelling back and forth."

Rin'urda brightened. "Would the Sentinals do that? The commander was suggesting a monthly service, but it would take too long and the information would be too old."

Birlerion called Ari. "There are the Arifels, too. I wonder if he will hear you if you call him."

"What is an Arifel?"

The air before them shimmered, and Ari popped into view, a bundle of black and brown fur with huge green eyes, scaly wings and tail. Rin'urda jerked back, and Birlerion coaxed Ari onto his hand.

"This is Ari. Don't be afraid. He is harmless. He carries messages for us. Ari, this is Rin'urda, one of Oscar's men."

Ari chittered, and Birlerion placed him in Rin'urda's hand. Rin'urda froze.

"He likes his ears rubbed."

Rin'urda hesitantly extended a finger and rubbed an ear.

Ari crooned and nuzzled his hand. Birlerion grinned as Rin'urda relaxed, mesmerised by the little creature.

"Let's see if he will hear you. Ask him to go to Kayerille. Just think the instruction in your mind and picture Kayerille."

Ari ignored Rin'urda and continued to rub against his fingers.

"Worth a try. They generally only hear guardians. They were the Lady's messengers. Not always reliable, but Ari has always come when I called, or his mate, Lin." Birlerion rubbed his chin. "Maybe we should ask him to check in periodically. There isn't always going to be a Sentinal to call him, especially when Versillion and I leave."

"Even if he pops in, he won't hear what I need him to do."

"We'll speak with Kayerille. Ari will carry messages. If we train him to pick up a message from a certain place, it won't matter. He can take it to Kayerille, and as long as you put a direction on the message, she can tell him where to go. It's not ideal; maybe you can think of a better way. That's the best I can think of at the moment."

Ari chittered and popped out of view, and Rin'urda rose. "I'll see what I can come up with. I'll go and plan out a schedule for the Sentinal network and suggest it to the commander. That might work well." Rin'urda talked to himself as he walked back to the office, and Birlerion grinned. It looked like Oscar had got lucky with his assistant.

Later that afternoon, Birlerion snared Oscar as he passed. "If none of you have anything better to do than watch me, you might as well come and talk to me."

Oscar grinned and sat down, accepting a glass of iced mint tea from Dar'ille, who had appointed himself Birlerion's main overseer.

"I'm glad to see you are being sensible at last. Sparring

was irresponsible, considering your condition. I'm surprised at you, Birlerion."

"You shouldn't be. We're all crazy Sentinals, remember? Out of place and out of time, with nowhere to call home."

"Is that what you want? A home?"

Birlerion rubbed his eyes. "I don't know what I want."

Oscar's voice was gentle. "You haven't had a chance to adjust, Birlerion. How are you supposed to know what you want? You've been awake a year, and you haven't stopped. You've been pushed from one crisis to the next and suffered major trauma. You need to rest, give yourself time. Instead, what are you doing? Charging across a burning desert as if nothing has happened."

"It's what I do best."

"No, it's what you *have* been doing, not what you have to *keep* doing. It's time to stop for a moment and just breathe. I think you need to take some time for yourself."

"I will once I've found Kino."

"Kino?"

"My horse."

"Ah, yes, your Darian. How can we help?"

A slow smile spread over Birlerion's face. "That's what I love about you, Oscar. You're always there when you're needed."

Oscar grinned. "We're friends, I hope. Of course I'm here for you. What do you need?"

"I need to go to Fuertes. I could use a couple of your men as extra guards as I need to go through Kirshan lands and I think the Kirshans may be the root of my trouble."

"Of course. I said you could have some of my men. I wouldn't let you go off into the desert on your own anyway."

Birlerion blinked and stared across the courtyard. "Thank you, Oscar."

"Anytime, Birlerion."

They sat in companionable silence as the sun sank behind the buildings and the brilliant blue of the sky deepened to a steel grey.

A messenger arrived with news that the Atolea had camped to the north of Mistra.

Birlerion smiled. "And the dance goes on."

"And you will be sitting this dance out," Oscar said. "They arrived faster than I expected."

"I can't sit it out. I need to speak to Maraine."

"You can speak to her tomorrow. You're not going anywhere today. You haven't stopped wheezing yet."

Birlerion twisted his lips. He had hoped Oscar hadn't noticed, but he should have known better.

"Send Kayerille, then. She knows Maraine."

"I was going to. She's useful to have around."

"And very pretty," Birlerion said with a smile.

Oscar snorted. "Beautiful, you mean, and dangerous. You two are close, aren't you?"

"We go way back. She almost joined with one of my best friends before the Lady sundered the stone. It wasn't to be."

"And what about you?"

"Me?"

"Aren't you and she … you know?"

Birlerion chuckled. "No. She thinks of me as her older brother."

"And are you happy with that?"

Birlerion considered Oscar. "If you are indicating your interest, then I should warn you that if you don't treat her right, I'll come looking for you."

Oscar grinned, his eyes bright. "Just a yes would have sufficed." He rose to his feet. "I'll ask her to mention you are here and you'll visit tomorrow. No carousing and no exercise. You stay here."

"Yes, Pa."

Oscar's laugh followed him into the building.

Birlerion observed the flurry of activity as Oscar selected two of his men to accompany Kayerille. He sighed as Versillion appeared beside him. "I keep my promises, you know. I haven't moved all day."

Versillion gripped his shoulder. "I know. Sometimes it is more difficult, though. Come and eat. You must be hungry."

"After doing nothing, you mean?" Birlerion said as he rose to follow Versillion across the courtyard to a dimly lit open area full of floor cushions and low tables.

"I've never known anyone to complain as much as you about having a day off. Just one day and you are a miserable sod."

"Is that what this was? You mean I've wasted my day sitting and doing nothing?"

Versillion laughed and pushed his brother onto a cushion.

Birlerion looked around the trellis-framed space. Pots of earth stood ready for the vines that he knew would be planted. He looked across at his brother. "This is nice. Why didn't you tell me this was here? I would have sat here all day."

"They've only just finished it. It's much nicer to dine al fresco than inside that dark building. The lads have got to have somewhere comfortable to relax when they are off duty."

"Whose idea was this?"

"Kayerille's."

"She is full of good ideas." Birlerion accepted the plate passed to him by one of the garrison staff, now proudly wearing a grey and black tabard over their robes denoting them as in the service of the King's Guards. Tucking in, he realised he was suddenly ravenous. "When were you out here then, Versillion? I don't remember you being posted to Terolia."

"You were in the cadets with Tagerill. I came out to the borders with Severen and Riss." Versillion laughed. "We were bumbling idiots, thought we knew it all, and came crashing down in our arrogance. That was why the Lady set up the outpost in Berbera; a staging point to acclimatise and get properly prepared.

"Riss suffered the worst. She had such pale skin. I remember her skin turning pink that first day. She was so pleased to get some colour for a change, and then that evening, she was on fire; her skin was scorching to the touch and the local Terolians had to help us cool her down." He looked at his plate. "A hard lesson learnt well. We covered up after that, but it did break the ice with the locals. They taught us how to survive. They were good people."

"They still are."

"Oscar is fortunate that he was welcomed here. He could have been seen as an intruder, but the Terolians have embraced the king and his policies."

Birlerion was silent.

Versillion gave him a sharp glance. "You don't think so?"

"I doubt every Terolian appreciates being absorbed by Vespiri. It will be interesting to hear what Maraine has to say. It's been nine, ten months since the conclave? Word will have percolated through to most by now. Remember, not all are affiliated with a Family, even though they speak for all. And the Kirshans didn't vote for it at all."

"That was nothing to do with the king."

"Cause and effect. It will be seen as a result of the king's interference. The conclave wouldn't have happened if the Captain hadn't turned up with the rest of us."

"Jerrol made that decision all on his own."

They stopped talking as they were joined by Ashton and

three of his men, who loosened their robes and relaxed onto the cushions, accepting the plates that the staff offered. Birlerion sipped his cold tea and stared up at the stars, thinking about the Kirshans. The soft voices lulled him, and he dozed.

Versillion shook his shoulder. "Why don't you go to bed, Birlerion? Let someone else use the cushions."

Birlerion rolled to his feet. "Sorry, I must have been more tired than I thought."

"Not surprising. Lady bless your sleep," Versillion said as he hugged him. Birlerion grinned at the men and retired to bed.

Birlerion dreamed he was riding across the desert on a honey-gold stallion, his robes and Kin'arol's black tail streaming behind them. They rode, free like the wind, as one, and he laughed. *I'm coming*, he thought, and a warm voice pervaded his dream: *I am here. I waited. I come to you.* And Birlerion opened his eyes.

The night was thick and velvety, a soft embrace pulling him back down into his slumber, but his eyes flicked open again at the sound of the slightest scuff. Silently, he felt for his dagger, peering through the darkness.

He rolled off his bed as a darker shadow pounced on him. He flung his arm up to block the strike. The blade sliced his bare skin, and he hissed as he scuttled back, the shadow following. His dagger slid down the sword and caught in the hilt as he was forced back against the wall. His left arm burned, but he blocked another strike, gripping the man's wrist. As his grip slipped, he desperately squeezed, ignoring the spike of pain. The man dropped the dagger and grunted as he brought his knee up into Birlerion's stomach.

Winded, Birlerion released his grip, and the man swung. Birlerion ducked, rolled away, and rose to his feet in a rather ragged motion. The man crowded him, and Birlerion staggered back. The man's momentum took them down in a swirl of robes as voices raised in alarm and people crowded into his room. Strong arms pulled the man off him, and he shuddered for breath as he tried to rise. His knees gave way as the adrenalin that had fuelled him, receded.

Versillion and one of Oscar's men forced him down onto the floor, trying to grab his flailing arms. He struggled to sit up, his body shaking as he grappled with his rescuers. "I can't breathe," he wheezed, and they jerked him upright as he desperately gasped for breath. Someone had grabbed his arm and was wrapping it, staunching the blood. Now that he had stopped fighting, his arm was on fire.

Oscar said from above him, "Kayerille, go ask Maraine if we can borrow her healer. Versillion, I want to find out everything you can about this man. I'll stay with Birlerion. Go on. Sergeant Ashton, I want to know how this assassin got past your guard. We will review our security protocols in the morning."

"Yes, sir."

The room slowly emptied, and Oscar crouched beside Birlerion as he wheezed on the floor. "I'm c-cold."

Oscar grabbed his robe and a blanket and wrapped Birlerion in them, hugging him close as he leant against the wall. Birlerion's breathing eased, and his panic subsided. "Well, that was an unexpected awakening," he whispered, shivering. Exhaustion overtook him, and he closed his eyes as he lay in Oscar's embrace. He dozed, his racing heart slowing as he relaxed.

"Is he alright?" A deep, motherly voice asked, and his eyes flew open.

"Maraine?" He tried to clear his throat and coughed. He

was unwrapped, and soft hands fluttered over him. "I'm fine. It's just a cut."

"You are not fine," a firm voice replied. "Medera, he needs to be moved to the camp. I can treat him better there."

"I just need a few stitches."

"Listen to the healer, Birlerion. She knows best. Here, drink. It will help soothe your throat." Oscar was insistent, and Birlerion drank the cool liquid and closed his eyes.

"What happened to him?" Maraine asked.

"Today? Or over the last three months?"

"All of it," the healer said.

Oscar recapped what he knew, and the healer looked at Birlerion again. "Move him now. These dank rooms are not helping him. They are not good for any of you."

When Birlerion awoke, he was lying in a vaulted tent. Golden lamps hung above him, bathing him in a warm glow. His arm was propped up on a pillow, and his upper body was raised by a stack of pillows.

He was back in a healerie, and the realisation made him sigh.

"Now, now, no need to be so despondent. You'll be out causing trouble soon enough if you as do as you're told and rest. Your arm needed twenty-five stitches, so let it recover." A young woman grinned at him, her black eyes sparkling in the lamplight. "As for the rest of you, those dank rooms were no good for your chest. You need dry heat, and we have plenty of that."

"Is that why I couldn't get rid of the wheeze?" he asked, sipping the liquid she presented to him.

"Partly, and time is the other. Injuries such as those you

suffered affect the whole body. It takes time for it all to realign and heal."

"It's been nearly four months."

"And it will take at least another four, so be patient."

Versillion's deep voice came from the door. "Patience has never been one of his virtues."

The healer smiled. "Then it's time he learned." She dipped her head and left.

"How are you feeling?" Versillion asked as he sat beside Birlerion.

"Still tired," Birlerion admitted.

"I suppose that's your body telling you to rest, so listen to it."

"What happened to my attacker?"

"The healer patched him up. He is Kirshan."

"But why do they want to kill me?"

"Someone must have heard you arrived in Terolia."

"But still, we've only been here a few days. They don't know our plans."

"Oscar's been scouring the garrison. He thinks one of the young boys on the staff was spying on us. He didn't turn up for work yesterday."

The healer returned with a tray of food. "Eat," she said. "I'll be in the outer room if you need me." Versillion stuffed another pillow behind Birlerion, who picked at the food.

Versillion watched him. "You'd better eat more than that or you won't be allowed out."

"I'm not hungry. I could do with some more water, though."

Versillion returned with the water, accompanied by Medera Maraine.

11

"Birlerion, you didn't have to attract assassins to Mistra to draw my attention," Maraine said as she sat beside him and grasped his hand. She was a tiny woman with sharp black eyes and dark brown hair coiled up on her head, giving her a few extra inches of height. She inspected him keenly.

"I can assure you I had no such intention," Birlerion said, squeezing her hand. She was the leader of the Atolea family. Her voice spoke for all, and she had declared that Birlerion was a son of the Atolea, honouring the decision of one of her ancestors from three thousand years ago. As a member, Birlerion could call on them for support at any time. And even though he hadn't asked for it, he was comforted by her concern.

"I know. Birlerion, you shouldn't be here. Your health is more important. You should be convalescing somewhere peaceful."

"I have been. It was driving me mad."

"Still, you are not strong enough to be going head-to-head with anyone."

"I just came to get my Darian."

"Yes, about that, I am so sorry. I thank you for the warning. It forestalled what could have been a difficult situation."

"I'm glad. It wasn't your fault."

"Maybe not directly, but I was the one on record proposing the removal of the Kirshan leaders. I suppose we should have expected some reprisals."

"Who are they proposing? I'm surprised they are still without a Medera."

Maraine sighed and stroked his hand. "There's too much infighting to be sure. I didn't think they had organised themselves enough to coordinate anything. I was mistaken. I am sorry, Birlerion. You have enough to deal with without this. I know how much he means to you. We've been looking for him, I swear."

"You won't find him without me; they've hidden him well. In Fuertes."

"But that is Solari territory. Why would they help the Kirshans?"

"Maybe they don't know they are."

Maraine stared at him. "How do you know he is there?"

Birlerion twisted his lips. "I know. But I need to go and find him or he is going to come and find me, and Lady knows how that will go." Birlerion took a deep breath. "He will do whatever he needs to do to reach me."

Maraine sat back and huffed. "Oh my, are you sure?"

"Yes, I am sure he is already trying to figure out how."

"You can hear him from Fuertes? That's unheard of."

Versillion chuckled. "Are you surprised?"

"I suppose not, but still, Fuertes? That's hundreds of miles away. That will take you weeks in your current condition. Could you use those waystone things?"

"He's not allowed. Marguerite forbade it."

"Marguerite?" Maraine said faintly.

"Yeah, she said he is not strong enough. He can't use them for three months."

"And you still came. Birlerion, you are a fool."

"I need him. He's mine."

Maraine observed Birlerion's stubborn face and patted his cheek. "Of course he is. No one else can bond with him; he can wait a little longer."

"No, he can't. They will keep trying to bond with him. They will be getting desperate now that they know I'm here. If he can't escape, I'm worried they might …" He faltered. "They might decide he's not worth the effort." He plucked at the light blanket covering him. "And I am stuck here."

Maraine considered him. "Then, if you promise to behave, we will take you to him. It's time I had a chat with the Kirshans. I'll take you as far as Rabat, and Lady knows, maybe he will meet you there if what you say is true."

"The Kirshans are looking for a fight," Birlerion said.

"They will regret posturing at me, I can assure you. I've been talking with your young commander. He's a sensible man. I've agreed to loan him some men to help train his."

Birlerion grinned. "You should consider making it a permanent arrangement. I think it would work better if the King's Guards are seen to include Terolians. And not just from the Atolea."

"You always have such interesting ideas, dear boy. I'll think about it."

Birlerion nodded and relaxed. "How's Viktor?" he asked, thinking of the elderly man who was Maraine's husband and Sodera.

"He is as well as can be expected. I expect he'll come and see you later."

"I'd be honoured," Birlerion replied.

Maraine leaned over and kissed his cheek. "Rest for now.

You'll soon be better." She rose, and Versillion escorted her out.

∼

Much later, Birlerion became aware that he was being watched. He opened his eyes and shifted his arm more comfortably on the cushion. The heat had worsened, and his skin was itching under the bandages.

He wiped his face on his sleeve and glanced around the tent. Intent black eyes peered at him from the corner. They disappeared for a moment, and then a small person wriggled under the canvas and slowly came forward.

Birlerion squinted at the child and then smiled as he recognised her. "Mir'elle?"

She bobbed her head and flipped her long hair out of her face. "You were here before," she said, "with the captain."

"Yes, that's right. You served us water."

She peered at him, pleased he remembered. "Do you need some now? I could get some for you."

"That would be very good of you. It is getting hot in here."

Mir'elle was back in a flash with a mug and a damp cloth. "Here." She proffered them both.

"You are very thoughtful. Thank you." He mopped his face and took a deep drink as she squatted beside him. She was a miniature Maraine, dainty yet with an underlying strength that surfaced as she squared her shoulders and met his eyes.

"Last time you were here, you showed the boys how to make a sling."

"Did they teach you?"

"They wouldn't, so I tried to copy them, but it won't work."

"Show me. Let's have a look."

She tugged her sling out from under her robes and, with some defiance, presented it.

"That is an excellent effort," he said as he inspected it. "It should work. Maybe it is the way you are using it. Show me." He handed the sling back, and she demonstrated her throw.

"Ah, I see. We need to shorten the length a little bit. You are losing your momentum. Do you have a knife?"

She brandished one.

"Ok, trim the ends and retie them." He watched her work; her deft handling of the knife was unsurprising, even at her age.

"Why wouldn't the boys show you how to make the sling?"

"They said I was too young. I'm seven! They are not much older."

"Then you are old enough. When I am better, I will show you how to use it properly. Have you had lessons on how to throw a knife?"

She shook her head.

Birlerion frowned. "It has a similar basis. We can start you on that, too."

Mir'elle flashed him a grateful smile, and Birlerion caught his breath at the glimpse of the beautiful woman she would become.

Placing his hand on his chest, he inclined his head. "The pleasure is mine," he said, keeping his face grave, and she giggled.

The healer peered through the doorway. "Mir'elle, what are you doing here? You know you are not supposed to enter the healerie."

"He was too hot."

"She has been no bother," Birlerion said at the same time.

The healer's lips quirked. "In that case, she can be useful and fill your jug with water."

Mir'elle scampered off, and when she returned, the healer gave her a large fan. "If you have nothing better to do, you may as well fan him. You are right; he is overheated."

Mir'elle and Birlerion exchanged glances, and Mir'elle began fanning him. Birlerion had to admit it felt good, though having the seven-year-old daughter of the Medera fanning him was a bit embarrassing. When she began to look a bit hot, they wrestled for the fan, and Birlerion fanned her for a while before they swapped again.

"When will you find your Darian?" she asked after a little while.

Birlerion stopped fanning in surprise. "How did you know I was looking for him?"

"Per'enne said."

"Per'enne?"

"My mare. She said he was sad."

"You shouldn't share her name with strangers, Mir'elle."

"You're my brother, and you've stopped fanning," she pointed out.

Birlerion chuckled at the tone of her voice and started fanning again.

"Mother said you were a son of the Family. I'm a daughter, so that makes you my brother."

"I am honoured to be named your brother," he said.

"The honour is mine," Mir'elle said and took the fan back.

"Your mare said he was sad?"

"Yes, he misses you."

"He's never met me."

"He should have by now. He knows."

"Knows?"

"That you're his." She tilted her head. "I think he is very lucky to have you."

Birlerion's heart clenched. "I think I am very lucky to have you as a sister." His heart melted at her brilliant smile.

The healer brought his dinner in, and Mir'elle was chased off to get her own. Birlerion started eating with a good appetite for once.

The next day, he was allowed up, though the healer strapped his arm against his chest so he couldn't use it. He was glad she helped him dress first; the thought of having his arm strapped under the robe made him sweat. He listened to her instructions and nodded dutifully before escaping with her warnings ringing in his ears.

The Atolean camp was busy, and he drifted through the laughing voices and bright faces, searching for a face he knew. He was surprised that he recognized so few, and then he stopped. Subconsciously, he had been thinking he would find Tiv'erna and his brothers; of course, he wouldn't know the Atoleans of today. He stared at the line of horses. He had found his way to the Darians. But again, there would be no Kaf'enir, She'velle, or Kin'eril.

An elegant grey mare nickered, and he moved nearer, offering her his hand. The mare blew over his hand and nudged him. He stroked a hand down her silky-smooth neck, and his tension eased.

I miss them, he thought, inhaling the musky scent of the mare's skin. Comfort emanated from her, and he bent his head against hers as he rubbed her chin.

He looked up, blinking away tears as a movement caught his eye. A skinny young lad dumped a bucket on the ground and offered him a small bag. "She likes the baliweed."

Birlerion gave the boy a weak grin. "They all like the baliweed. My mare used to complain that I didn't stock enough of it."

"They are greedy. They don't need it all the time. It wouldn't be a treat if they had it every day."

"Wise words," Birlerion said as he awkwardly opened the bag.

"Sorry. I should have opened it. I didn't realise you …" The lad trailed off. "Oh. It's you. No wonder she likes you." He stooped and picked up the bucket before scampering off.

Birlerion tilted his head as he offered the mare the scented grass. "Now, what was that supposed to mean?" She whuffled over his hand and then nudged him for more.

"Didn't you hear what he said? You don't need too much. It's a treat." He gripped the bag in his teeth, sprinkled a few stalks in her net, and grinned as she dove into it.

"I might have known I'd find you here," Kayerille said from behind him. "Are you trying to steal that mare?"

Birlerion spat the bag out of his mouth, the aromatic scent of green herbs and sweet anise lingering in his nose. "As if. Kino would be very upset, though she is a beauty."

"Maraine sent me to find you."

Birlerion turned away from the mare. "What's the date, Kayerille? I've lost track."

"It is the thirtieth of Augu. Year of our Lady 4125."

"No wonder it's so hot," he said, dabbing his face with the edge of his robe. "I seem to have lost a few days here and there."

"Along with a few thousand years. A few days won't make much difference." Kayerille's laugh was sour. "Not surprising, I suppose."

Birlerion halted at the bitterness in her voice. "What's the matter?"

"Why should something be the matter?"

"You tell me."

"You're impossible. You know that?"

"Me?"

"Yes, you. You almost die and then you rush out here and almost get yourself killed. What are the rest of us supposed to do without you?"

"Whoa, hang on a minute, Kayerille. What do I have to do with anything?"

"You're my only family, Birlerion. I don't want to be on my own."

Birlerion carefully hugged her. "You don't have to be on your own. You'll make your own family."

"I'm afraid to," she admitted, resting her head on his shoulder. She wrapped her arms around his waist, desperately seeking comfort, her voice low. "What if I lose them, like Lily, Daniel, Mattie, and … and Tiv'erna. I don't think I could live through that again."

"Kayerille …" Birlerion hesitated, feeling her anguish. "You can't spend your life worrying about what-ifs. You have a second chance. Make the most of it."

"Yeah, like you are?"

"I'm trying. I admit it's not easy, but Tiv'erna would not have wanted you to stop living because he is not here. I can hear him now; he would be cheering you on. You won't love him less for loving someone else."

Oscar's sharp voice interrupted them. "Hey, lovebirds, stop canoodling. The Medera is waiting."

They broke apart and the moment shattered. Kayerille flushed as she turned away and pushed past Oscar and into the tent. Oscar glared at Birlerion as he followed her through the flap.

12

Maraine patted the cushions beside her. "Kayerille, Birlerion, come sit. We need to discuss our journey to Rabat. Commander Landis and I have agreed that we will exchange four men, mine to support his garrison and provide training, his to accompany us to Rabat in their place; the beginnings of the Terolian King's Guards, as you suggested." She smiled at Oscar, who sat opposite.

His smile was frigid.

"That is excellent news, Maraine," Birlerion said, drawing Maraine's attention from Oscar, hoping to give him time to recover his composure. "And what are the plans for travelling to Rabat?"

"We'll head to Marmera first and then cut across to Koav and then to Rabat before turning north."

"Will Medera Reina be in Fuertes?"

"I have sent word on ahead. I expect her to be by the time we get there."

"Are you sure about this, Maraine? You'll be a prime target, heading into Kirshan territory. Wouldn't it be better for a small group of us to travel?"

Maraine patted his hand. "My dear boy, I should be able to travel anywhere in Terolia, and if I cannot, then that is a matter for the conclave to resolve, not you." She sat up. "Now, this is the hot season. Viktor will remain here in camp with the children and those who should not travel. Oscar will extend his protection over my camp, for which I thank him. We will leave as soon as your arm is out of the sling and the healer clears you to ride. I need you fit to fight if necessary."

"Of course, Medera."

"Good. We will spend the next week paring back the camp and readying for travel. Viktor needs to speak to you regarding the life debt. You are a son of the Atolea and you were attacked by a Kirshan."

Birlerion stiffened. "Maraine, no, he didn't get close to killing me. There is no life debt."

"According to Family Law, it is the intent, not the result, that determines the debt. You are owed, Birlerion. He attempted to take your life, without justification to do so."

"But you were not responsible for my safety, and the king does not require a life for a life."

"He does in Terolia," Maraine said, her voice stern. "A Kirshan attacked you intending to take your life without cause. As a result of his action, he forfeited his life for yours. You will decree his punishment."

Birlerion bowed his head. "I'll speak to Viktor," he said, his reluctance plain.

"Do it now, Birlerion."

Kayerille reached for his arm but hesitated at his bleak expression. Oscar's face tightened as he observed her gesture. Birlerion rose and left the tent. He walked towards the black tent at the rear of the camp, his mouth dry.

He ducked under the flap and paused, adjusting to the dim light. The man was bound to the pole in the centre of the tent. The air was stifling and sweat dribbled down the man's face. He jerked to his feet as Birlerion entered, and Viktor rose from his chair.

"The law decrees a life for life. Bal'enna of Kirsha offers no mitigating excuse. He states his intent was and still is to kill Birlerion, son of the Atolea. He admits to the attempt to assassinate Birlerion on the night of the twenty-fifth of Augu. I, Viktor, Sodera of the Atolea, ask Birlerion, son of the Atolea, to pronounce his judgement."

Birlerion approached the man, who straightened in defiance and stared at him with hatred in his black eyes.

"Why did you try to kill me?"

The man sneered. "You dare to walk the lands of Terolia when you betray the Family. You do not deserve to live."

"Says who?"

The assassin was silent. His black eyes narrowed.

"Why did you steal my Darian? Where is he?"

"Silver-eyed Betrayer," the man spat.

"Whom have I betrayed?"

Silence.

"If there is an accusation against my name, by law I have a right to know."

More silence.

"The Kirshans cannot kill arbitrarily. I have a right of response."

The man hissed, straining at his restraints and Viktor gripped Birlerion's shoulder.

"You have a choice," Birlerion said, "banishment or death."

"There is no difference. Banishment *is* death. You are nothing more than an executioner at the beck and call of the Atolea."

"No," Birlerion replied. "Your choice brought us here. You are the executioner. There is a difference. You can claim mercy and die quickly, or you can suffer and die slowly; the choice is yours."

The man's laugh was harsh. "You think you offer mercy? Then *you* do it. You are the hand that wealds the knife, or I walk. And my suffering will be on your head. You choose. Either way, my blood is on your hands."

"No," Viktor said, his voice cold, "your blood is on your own hands and no others. The debt is paid." He struck, driving the blade up under the man's ribs and into his heart. The man spluttered, and as if held by strings, he slowly rotated around the pole and collapsed.

Birlerion grabbed Viktor as he stumbled, twisting awkwardly to hold him up. The guard leapt forward, took Viktor's weight, and eased him back into his chair. Birlerion knelt beside him, his heart beating rapidly. "Viktor, you didn't have to do that."

"Yes, I did. I am an old man. I have dealt justice before, and there was no need for his vitriol to bother you any longer than necessary. The debt is paid." He leaned his head back and breathed in deeply. "It would not have done you any good to have dealt the blow. You have seen enough death already."

"The Lady expects us to protect, and if that means killing, then we kill so others don't have to."

"Exactly," Viktor said. "My son, you honour us by your vigilance, but this was my duty. All I ask is that you protect the Medera in my place. I can ask no other. To do so would admit to my weakness and undermine her. It is not time for her to step down; there is so much still to be done."

Birlerion glanced at the guard standing over them.

"Do not worry about Per'serre. He will not betray us. In fact, this night will extend my reputation for a while longer."

Birlerion gave Viktor a faint smile. "In that case, I am glad to have been of service, Sodera."

Viktor chuckled. "That's the spirit. Now, let us return to my dear wife and relieve her of her worries. I feel like a drink."

Per'serre escorted them back to the Medera's tent and eased Viktor into his chair next to her. Maraine fussed over him until Viktor shooed her away. "Stop fussing, woman. You'll have them thinking I can no longer dispense justice."

Maraine stopped and stared at him.

"The debt is paid," he said softly.

Maraine swivelled to Birlerion.

"The debt is paid," he said, "and the Sodera deserves a drink."

Per'serre returned with a silver flask and a tray of glasses, and Maraine sat down. Kayerille held her hand over her mouth, and Oscar stared at them, bewildered. Per'serre poured the drinks and handed the tray around, taking the final glass for himself. "To justice," he pronounced.

"To justice," Birlerion repeated and knocked the drink back, trying not to choke as his eyes watered.

"To justice," Kayerille repeated, her eyes tearing before she had even taken a drink.

Viktor grinned. "To justice," he said and turned his empty glass over on the table. Maraine's slapped down next to his, and they turned to Oscar.

"It's better just to knock it back," Birlerion advised. "It tastes awful if you sip it."

"I'm not sure what I'm drinking to," Oscar said.

"Necessity," Birlerion said sadly, "something you will have to acquaint yourself with out here."

"Whose necessity was it to kill a man? I assume you did kill him?"

"Family Law must be upheld or it means nothing," Birlerion replied.

"There are rules and procedures. You can't just take justice into your own hands," Oscar protested.

"The rules were followed. Clemency was offered, and it was declined. Justice follows," Viktor said, his face stern.

"You are in Terolia now. Family Law applies," Birlerion said.

Oscar placed his full glass on the table and stood. "Terolia is part of Vespiri now, so the King's Law applies." He bowed to Maraine and Viktor. "Medera, Sodera, Sentinal Kayerille." He turned and left the tent.

There was a short silence, and Viktor grimaced. "It appears the young commander is an idealist. I will endeavour to instruct him whilst you are gone. Shall we have another drink? I think I might need it."

Per'enne poured another round, and Birlerion and Kayerille saluted each other before downing their drinks and spluttering.

"Viktor," gasped Birlerion, "you have to find something else. This is disgusting. No wonder Oscar didn't want to drink it."

"Only a true Terolian will drink it. It's how you know who you are dealing with," Viktor said with a grin.

13

B irlerion accosted Oscar as he crossed the courtyard garrison the next morning. "We need to talk."

"About what?"

"About last night."

"There is nothing to discuss."

"Oscar, you misunderstand."

"It's Commander Landis to you."

"Oscar, please. I told you. Kayerille is like my sister; we comfort each other. You don't know what it's like to feel so alone. Sometimes it overwhelms you."

"You are not alone. You have family everywhere. Versillion is here, and the Atolea."

Birlerion stared at him, and Oscar swallowed at the taut expression on his face. "I was referring to Kayerille," Birlerion said at last and turned away.

Oscar didn't get the chance to speak to him again before they left a week later. Birlerion nodded at him from his position beside the Medera, his face guarded. He had retreated behind his considerable reserve, and Oscar didn't know how to break it down. As he watched them leave, deep down, he knew he had said the wrong thing. Still, his anger at Birlerion's deceit stiffened his resolve. Birlerion had said he had no interest in Kayerille, obviously a lie. His gaze slid over Kayerille as she watched Birlerion and the others ride away. The expression of concern on her face galled him. He turned his back and re-entered the garrison.

Rin'urda was waiting for him, and Oscar heaved a sigh. Rin'urda was determined to prove that he was an excellent assistant. Not only had he set up the Sentinal network, travelling by waystone with Kayerille and suffering the indignity of throwing up his guts at each location, he was also proving to be more knowledgeable than expected.

"I have more information on the Kirshans."

"Tell me," Oscar said as he sat behind his desk.

"It appears that Medera Silva has managed to retain her position as Medera of the Kirshans."

"What?"

"Look." Rin'urda spread out some papers on Oscar's desk.

"Reports have just come in. The Kirshans have refused to choose a new Medera. They claim they already have one."

"Do you know where they are?"

"Difficult to tell. Last known camp was east of Marmera."

Oscar scowled. "That is near the route the Medera intends to take. Too near."

"I sent a request for more information about the whereabouts of Sir'elo, her son. If anyone is going to cause trouble, it would be him."

"Well done." Oscar leaned back in his chair. "Rin'urda, I just wanted to say what a good job you are doing."

Rin'urda flushed.

"I know we didn't start off too well, but I honestly don't think I could cope without you."

"Sir, that was my fault, not yours. You opened my eyes to

what I should have been doing. We have so much more visibility now. It is amazing."

Oscar grinned. "So, you are happy to be the adjutant to the commander of the Terolian King's Guard?"

"Oh, yes, sir."

"What about the Mistran local security?"

"About that, sir ..."

Oscar grinned as his adjutant outlined his plans to promote his assistant.

"Is everything alright?"

Oscar glanced up from his paperwork, glad for the interruption. However, when he realised who had interrupted him, he wasn't so sure. Kayerille hovered in his doorway as glints of gold from his lamp highlighted her night-black hair and burnished her beautiful face. "Of course," he said, and he threw down his quill and leaned back in his chair.

Her smile warmed his heart as she sat in the chair opposite him. "Good. From the way you were scowling, I thought something terrible had happened."

Oscar snorted. "I hate paperwork; it never ends."

"Delegate it to someone who likes doing it, then."

"I doubt half my men can write, let alone organise."

"You are a commander now. You should have an assistant."

"I do, but he still generates paperwork. And anyway, I'm not a real commander. Sentinal Birlerion made that up."

"Once the king gets your report, I am sure he will ratify it. You have worked wonders here, Oscar, and it's only been a couple of weeks. Imagine what you can do over time."

Oscar stiffened. "Was there a reason you came visiting or was this just a social call?"

Kayerille's smile slipped. "I came to check if you needed me tomorrow."

"No, I don't believe we do. Medera Maraine's men will take over the training. Thank you for your help up till now."

Kayerille tilted her head, observing him. "Very well. You know where I am if you need me." She rose. "You will let me know if you hear any news from the Medera."

"Of course," Oscar said, gritting his teeth. "As should you if you hear anything first."

He stared at the door as she left. She only wanted to stick around for news of Birlerion. He should have known better. He bent back over his paperwork. A few minutes later, he cursed and threw his quill down. Rising, he left his office and looked out over the garrison.

It seemed empty without the Sentinals. One of them was usually in the sparring ring, their presence larger than life. There was just something different about them. He sighed. What was he doing, mooning over a Sentinal he couldn't have? He had more important things to do.

He turned as Dar'ille approached. "Do you have the personnel files on the staff?" Oscar asked. He didn't think they would tell him anything, but he wanted to know who they were affiliated with. He should have done that from the start. He had allowed Birlerion to lull him into relying on the security of Family Law. He hadn't realised it was so ingrained until Birlerion's recent demonstration. Though he supposed he should have known.

Dar'ille handed over a stack of paper, and Oscar retreated to his office. Before Birlerion returned, he would find out who had tried to kill him and why. His garrison would be secure. He frowned over the papers.

An hour later, he tossed them away. They weren't worth the paper they were written on. He sat staring at the wall. No matter how angry he was, he couldn't sit by and allow a

Sentinal to be killed, especially not Birlerion. He sighed and rubbed his eyes. He liked him. Birlerion said he was a friend. Oscar didn't have that many friends, and friends were worth preserving. If only he could get past Kayerille. He stood up and paced; he wasn't sure he could.

He stiffened. If there were no Kayerille, he wouldn't be hesitating. Lady help him. He left his office. "Sanderson, with me." He strode down the street towards the Atolean camp.

The guard ushered them in, and Oscar hesitated as he spotted Kayerille. He approached her. "Any chance you can get me an audience with Viktor?"

"Of course. Let me check." Kayerille ducked into the main tent, and a moment later, she came out and beckoned him forward.

"Wait here," he murmured to Sanderson and entered the tent. He paused and inclined his body as he caught Viktor's eye. "Sodera, I appreciate you taking the time to see me so quickly."

Viktor raised an eyebrow. "So formal when we have just waved off a joint venture."

Oscar grimaced. "About that, I think we may have made a mistake."

"What do you mean?"

"I think the theft of Birlerion's Darian had nothing to do with him."

Kayerille gasped. "What?"

"I think the true target is Maraine or you, Viktor." He grimaced again. "Or both of you."

"Why?"

"Because no one knew Birlerion would be coming to Terolia. He didn't know himself until a few weeks ago. There is no connection to him whatsoever. If Birlerion is not the connection, then the only other link is the Atolea. Versillion told me that Birlerion was worried about the implications for the Atolea, that's why he insisted on travelling now. If he could find his Darian, then the agreement would be upheld."

Viktor tutted. "That boy knows far more than he should. If they didn't know he was coming here then why attack him?"

"Because he is affiliated to you and you would respond as you have."

"Birlerion was concerned about the effect the theft would have on you," Kayerille said, frowning in thought. "He thought the Atolea would suffer, that Maraine's rule would be called into question."

"Birlerion always had a deep understanding of Family Law," Viktor said with a slight smile.

"You are saying Birlerion is just collateral damage?" asked Kayerille.

Oscar waggled his hand. "I'm not sure. It was only a month or so ago that we knew Birlerion was even alive and recovering. Who would have known in Terolia? I had no idea he would turn up here. I don't see how stealing his horse had anything to do with him; it was to do with the Atolea. It is just their bad luck that he is here."

"So, the Kirshans attacked Birlerion before he could make a difference?"

"I think it was a spur-of-the-moment decision that didn't succeed."

Viktor pondered for a moment. "It is possible, though I would suggest I am the easier target."

Kayerille glanced at him and back to Oscar. "Commander Landis, what do you suggest?"

"There is little we can do except protect Viktor. We can at least make him less of an easy target."

"What of your staff? Do you trust them?"

"As much as I can trust anyone. They have no reason to be loyal to me."

"Then we work around them." Kayerille crouched next to Viktor and held his hand. "Birlerion will protect Maraine. It's you we need to worry about."

Landis stared at her. "You have great faith in him."

Kayerille grinned, her eyes alight. "You should never underestimate a Sentinal, especially not Birlerion."

Viktor chuckled. "She's right. Do you know how old he was when he first came to Terolia and changed our history?"

"You mean when he saved my life?" Kayerille said with a small smile.

Viktor patted her hand. "He was eighteen. Do you know how old he is now?" Viktor paused. "No? Just turned twenty. And still saving the world."

"Give or take three thousand years," Kayerille muttered.

"Exactly. He is touched by the Lady, as are you, my dear." Viktor observed Oscar's expression, and he leaned forward and stared Oscar in the eye. "If I had the choice of anyone protecting my wife, it would be him."

"You make him seem invincible."

"Oh, no!" Viktor exclaimed. "I wish he was. He is tenacious. He is a Lady's Guard, and he embodies her spirit."

"We protect those who cannot protect themselves," Kayerille said.

"Until death," Viktor said, his face sad.

Oscar stilled. "What aren't you telling me?"

"Nothing you don't know already. Birlerion is stubborn, but the injuries he took at Oprimere are not fully healed. Versillion said he nearly died, and his lungs are still causing him problems. He shouldn't be here."

"Then why did you let him go?"

"Because he came to rescue his Darian, and he won't leave without him."

"I don't understand. Couldn't someone else search for him?"

"Only Birlerion can bond with his Darian," Kayerille said as she stood. "Sodera, we need to fortify the camp."

"Commander Landis will protect us," Viktor said. "Together we will hold them off until Maraine reaches the Solari. The Mederas will resolve this Kirshan issue."

Oscar stared at him in disbelief. They were all crazy.

Oscar heard the buzz without recognising it at first. He opened his eyes from his heat-of-the-day doze and sat up, searching. Another buzz whizzed past his ear, and he watched it fly out of the garrison gate and straight down the road towards the older part of the city. It was late afternoon, and the sun was low in the sky; the day was still baking hot. It had been three days since Birlerion had left, and still no word. Oscar rose, and after straightening out his robes, he picked up his canteen and walked out of the garrison.

Fer'ilan, one of the young Atoleans assigned to the garrison, caught the duty-sergeant's eye, and at the jerk of his head, he followed the commander at a discreet distance. The commander didn't appear to be following a direct route and often paused, usually near a flowering cactus or trailing vine. He consistently worked his way towards the older sector, and he finally paused near the stone fountain of the Lady outside the temple and stared at the brilliant crimson vine draping the small building. It was festooned with long, tubular yellow flowers, and tiny bees crawling among the blooms.

Oscar jerked around as a door opened behind him and Kayerille stepped into the street. The sun's rays burnished her silver-green robes so that they shimmered like sparkles on a calm sea.

She cocked an eyebrow at him, her hand on the temple door. "Were you looking for me?" She searched the street, and a crease appeared between her brows. "You didn't come alone, did you?" She spotted Fer'ilan as he deliberately moved, and she relaxed.

"I was following the bees," Oscar said. "I hadn't noticed the flowers. The desert is so bare; you forget that such beautiful plants exist, along with the creatures that nurture them."

Kayerille's face softened. "There is beauty everywhere. Sometimes you have to look a little harder to find it."

"True," he murmured, watching the busy bees.

"Why were you following the bees?" she asked from beside his shoulder, and he shivered.

"When I was a youth, I helped look after bees. I collected the honey and wax. We were trying to introduce wax candles, but we didn't have enough bees to make it worthwhile."

"Ah, I see. You were a pioneer, trying to rid the world of tallows."

Oscar chuckled. "I believe that is a fine aspiration. They were never my favourite."

"No, I must admit, here in Terolia, we prefer oil lamps. They still smell but not so much."

Oscar turned away from the flowers. "Now that you mention it, there aren't many candles here, are there?"

"No, we only use them when travelling. Once in camp, lamps are used." She gave him a quick grin. "Or an onoff, of course. If you could get your hands on one. They were priceless."

"An onoff?"

"The Lady used to make them for the scholars. Safer than a naked flame, apparently. Birlerion told me about them once. A golden ball of light suspended in the air."

"I've never heard of it. Are you sure he wasn't pulling your leg?"

"Pulling my leg?"

"Tricking you, making you believe something that wasn't true."

"Birlerion would not lie about the Lady," she said, her face grave.

"I suppose not. It does sound a bit unlikely, though."

"You don't know Birlerion very well, do you?"

Oscar bristled. "And you do?"

A small smile played around her mouth. "Some." She scanned their surroundings. "Did you intend to visit the temple or do you wish to follow more bees?"

Oscar tamped down his irritation. "I think I'll return to the garrison. Would you be able to resume your training tomorrow? Your technique is different. It would be good for the men to learn to fight against variations."

"Of course. I'll help in any way I can."

"Good. I'll see you in the morning, then." Oscar nodded and retraced his steps, his irritation fading into contentment. He didn't stop to consider why; he just enjoyed the feeling. He was sure it wouldn't last.

14

Struggling to tie his spare scarf around Narell's head, Birlerion hung on for dear life as the ferocious wind tugged at his clothes. He fought to hold onto his flimsy scarves as he pulled them up across his eyes and hid his face in Narell's neck. It was every man and woman for themselves as the wind howled around them, flinging sand in every direction and making it impossible to see.

The buffeting wind scattered them as men tried to restrain the squealing animals as the sandstorm scoured its way through them. Hunkering down, Birlerion coughed as the grit worked its way through his scarves.

When the winds died down and the leading edge of the storm had swept its way eastwards, Birlerion eased his scarves away and peered into the murky air. The light was dim; the sun was still shrouded by the dust hanging in the air. Peculiar shadows rose from the ground. The edges blurred in the false light.

Coughing in the dust-laden air, Birlerion led his horse towards the shadows.

Versillion's hoarse voice penetrated the gloom. "Birlerion?"

"Yeah." Birlerion inhaled and started coughing again. Versillion grabbed him and his horse's reins. "Keep your face covered."

If Birlerion could have stopped coughing, he would have told his brother not to state the obvious. His coughing did bring the others to them, though. Val'eria, Maraine's healer, squatted beside him and offered him her canteen as he tried to clear his throat.

Maraine loomed beside him. "We need to get him out of this dust." She squinted into the desert. The sun was high, a perfect golden ball suspended above them. "Koav is nearest."

"I'm fine," Birlerion croaked and promptly started coughing again.

"No, you aren't," Versillion said. "This dust is killing you." He unravelled Birlerion's scarves and tried to shake them out before wrapping them back around his face. He helped Birlerion back on his horse and looked up at him with concern. Birlerion bent forward, holding his chest as he tried to suppress the spasm of coughing that shook him.

Versillion held onto the reins of Birlerion's horse and led him over to his own horse. Mounting, he followed Ran'eder and Maraine into the gloom, surrounded by Maraine's men. The desert was eerily quiet, as if everything living thing had hunkered down and was waiting for the dust to settle. The hollow echo of Birlerion's coughing followed them through the gloom.

The village of Koav emerged from the dull yellow light, just where it was supposed to be. It was situated in the lee of the Kharma Ridge, which rose to their left, forming an impenetrable barrier of rock down the centre of Terolia. They veered towards the village, ignoring Birlerion's breathless protests.

Koav had once been a large town. It was now a small

village clinging to the edge of a thready tributary of the Kharma River. The river had long since disappeared, sinking into the rock strata below and leaving a wide, dry riverbed. It resurfaced on the plains of Fuertes to the north, wending its way through lush grasses grazed on by the Darian herd nurtured by the Solari and the Gusars before emptying into the sea.

The once-rich arable land had shrunk to the edges of the tributary, where spiky crops grew and spindly olive trees clung tenaciously to bare rock. Families lived in the caves carved out of the valley walls, sheltered from the heat and storms. Many more were empty.

The village was deserted; everyone was still battened down, waiting out the storm. Ran'eder led them to one of the empty caves, and Birlerion was escorted into the dim interior. He sat and pulled off his scarves so he could sip his water. His shoulders shook as he suppressed a cough.

"Medera, if you would wait here until we erect the camp," Ran'eder said.

Maraine glanced over at Birlerion. "I think he'll be better in here than a tent."

"Of course, but you will be safer in our camp. We cannot defend you in here."

"Very well, but we'll be travelling on to Rabat tomorrow."

Birlerion's head ached, and his chest hurt. He was so fed up with feeling ill. Every time he thought he had recovered, he had a relapse. He felt like he was dragging himself through quicksand, and he was sinking fast. "I'm sorry, Maraine. I shouldn't have come with you."

"You were doing fine, Birlerion. It's not your fault we met a sandstorm."

The cave echoed with his cough, and the young healer's

assistant, Val'eria, hurried in. "Here, take this. It will relax your muscles and help your chest. The grit must have got into your lungs." She knelt beside Birlerion and offered him a phial.

Birlerion grimaced but knocked it back. Intent dark-brown eyes watched him, and she relaxed as he did. "Rest. You will be fine tomorrow."

"Thanks, Val'eria," Birlerion said and closed his eyes. She tucked a rug around him, and Maraine sat beside him.

"What do you think the Kirshans are up to?" Maraine asked, resting her chin in her hand.

Birlerion opened his eyes. "Ultimately? They want their star to rise."

"But they are going about it the wrong way. All they had to do was vote in a new Medera and they would be back in the fold."

"From what Virenion said, there is no hope of that happening anytime soon, which makes this venture even riskier for you."

"There was no point in stopping in Marmera, no matter what Virenion said. Your Darian is in Fuertes, as is Reina, and I can't be seen to be afraid of the Kirshans."

"But there is no point in taking unnecessary risks. The Kirshans are unpredictable. They are leaderless, and their young hotheads are going to cause us problems." He flicked a glance at her. "I asked Virenion to go to Fuertes and ask Medera Reina to meet us in Rabat."

Maraine sat up. "You did what?"

"There is more going on than the Kirshans stealing my horse, and it is more than an Atolean issue. You need support."

"That was not your decision to make, Birlerion."

He lifted his head and stared at the wall. Something wasn't right. He rose, coughing hollowly. "Stay out of sight," he said as he wrapped the scarves around his face. He drew his sword and peered out of the cave. Two of Maraine's men guarded the entrance. The rest were setting up camp.

The skeleton of the tent was up, and men were hauling the canvas over the frame. Dust still hung in the air, shimmering in the heat. A shout went up, and the horses stirred on the picket line.

Before the men could react, a horde of horses charged the men, scimitars slashing. Men swirled, their swords flashing, and the tent collapsed, adding to the confusion. Birlerion tensed as Versillion dragged a horse forward and charged into the melee. More steel clashed, and men shouted as bodies slumped to the sand.

"See if you can get some horses," Birlerion instructed the guards before ducking back into the cave. "We need to move. It looks like the Kirshans have decided to act."

Maraine stood, her face calm. "We cannot leave. If they are here for me, they will not stop until they find me."

"They may not know you are here, and I am not handing you over to them. They are out of control, Maraine, and there is no way you are going out into that."

"Of course they know I'm here. They must have been following us."

"They will kill you, Maraine. This is not the time to be stubborn. Come on." He pulled her to the doorway and peered out. Dust swirled, confusing the scene.

Birlerion thought fast. If he could get her to Rabat, Illiserille could hide her in her sentinal. Ran'eder rode out of the dust, one of his men close behind him. "The Medera," he gasped, and Birlerion shoved her up in front of him, ignoring her protests.

"Find Sentinal Illiserille!" he shouted and turned to cover their retreat. He gritted his teeth as a horse charged straight for him.

"Birlerion?"

"Kin'arol? They attack the Medera. Send help."

"Where are you?"

Birlerion staggered as he blocked a strike, which vibrated through his body. He spun and threw his dagger. The man lurched in his saddle, and Birlerion turned and ran towards the swirling dust.

"Birlerion?"

"Koav."

"I come."

"No, Kin'arol, no."

He stumbled as the dust overwhelmed him, his chest spasming, and then he blindly tripped over a body, dropping to his knees as a sword hummed overhead. Regaining his feet, he cut diagonally away from the collapsed tent, towards the village. Drumming feet behind him made him turn, and he parried the slashing blade. Twisting, he gripped the rider's arm, and his momentum dragged the man out of his saddle and his arm almost out of its socket. Birlerion pounced, his knife at the man's throat, his shoulder burning. "Who are you?" he asked, coughing.

"Your death," the man spat, his black eyes glittering.

"By a coward who has no name and no honour?" Birlerion replied. Twisting his knife, he pulled the man's scarf off, the ridged tattoo of Kirsha adorned the man's face.

The Kirshan laughed and glanced over Birlerion's shoulder. Birlerion didn't hesitate; he pulled the man around, shielding himself, and the sword thrust impaled the Kirshan instead. Birlerion let the man go, and as he slumped to the sand, his dead weight fouled the blade, ripping it out of the other Kirshan's hand. The rider cursed and pulled out his short sword. "If you want your men to live, you will surrender now and hand over the Medera."

"Now, why would I do that?" Birlerion asked, straightening as he stared at the man.

The man's black eyes glanced around. His face was hidden by swathes of brown scarves. He gripped his reins tightly. His body was tense, and the bay-coloured Darian jinked uncomfortably. "You are one of them, the betrayers."

A shout behind Birlerion curdled his blood. "We've got him. The silver-eyed betrayer is dead." They could only mean Versillion.

"The Medera is in Mistra," he said as he called Ari.

"Then you will suffice," the man said. "Move." He gestured with his blade.

As Birlerion stepped over the body on the ground, he pulled out the sword. "Don't even think about it," the man snarled, and Birlerion walked back towards the camp, the sword gripped in hand.

He stopped as he reached what was left of their camp. Three of Maraine's men and two of Oscar's knelt in the sand, guarded by the Kirshans. Red-rimmed slashes stained their robes. Five out of twenty. Versillion lay awkwardly in front of them, unnaturally pale, and Birlerion's heart lurched.

"So, this is Kirshan honour," he said.

One of the Kirshans struck out at Birlerion. His fist glanced off Birlerion's cheek, and Birlerion collapsed to his knees as he bent over, coughing. The scimitar was wrenched out of his nerveless hand, and the prisoners watched as the sword was returned to its owner.

"Enough," the Kirshan said as he slid off his horse and sheathed his sword. He loosened his scarves, revealing a surprisingly young face. His black eyes glittered with determination. "Search him."

Birlerion was relieved of his remaining dagger and his

sling. He didn't fight them. Instead, he concentrated on breathing.

"Where is the Medera?"

"She's not here," Birlerion wheezed. "I told you, she is in Mistra." Birlerion rode the blow.

"This is the Medera's tent. Who are you to be given such treatment?"

Birlerion regained his knees. "Who are you to attack a legitimate Atolean patrol?"

"An Atolean patrol with two betrayers? I think you are not an ordinary patrol. Where is the Medera?"

"I told you, she is not here." Birlerion stiffened as one of the Kirshans dragged forward a struggling Val'eria. She twisted free an arm and the man cursed as her fist caught his face. Val'eria stilled as she saw the men on their knees, and the young Kirshan leader grabbed her. He held her against him, and with terrified eyes, she stared at Birlerion and the men. "We have been in the saddle for many days. A woman like this"—he groped her breast—"can help relieve the tension."

Birlerion stared at him in disgust. "Would you stoop so low? Have the Kirshans lost all honour?"

The man's grip tightened, and Val'eria paled.

Birlerion continued. "Your Medera betrayed her people, not the other Families. She sold you out to the Ascendants. They killed thousands of your people. Is that what you profess to honour? Murderers?"

"You lie." The Kirshan gripped Val'eria around the throat, and she struggled in his grip.

Birlerion chuckled and then coughed. "I was there. I saw your Medera unmasked." He changed tack at the expression on the man's face. "How many injured men do you have?" Birlerion asked. "I imagine this was an expensive venture."

"Who are you?"

"The woman you are strangling is a healer. Maybe her time would be better spent treating your men and mine. There is no need for anyone else to die here."

The man eased his grip. "Does he speak true?"

Val'eria jerked her head.

"What is his name?"

She shuddered, and the man's grip tightened.

"Sentinal Virenion," she croaked, her eyes downcast. Birlerion kept quiet and hoped none of the others would correct her. His name must be more well-known than he had thought if Val'eria felt the need to lie.

The man kicked Versillion. "And this one?"

"Sentinal Versillion."

A ripple of murmurs passed around the Kirshans, and the man released her. "Wake him up."

Val'eria dropped beside Versillion, and her hands fluttered over him. "I need my kit. His leg is broken."

"You can get it when you treat my men. Make do."

Val'eria grabbed a shattered tent pole and straightened his leg. Versillion groaned but didn't regain consciousness. "I need my kit to wake him."

"Rin'eta, take her to our men. She can treat them first. Then wake him up. Tie the rest up. Keep an eye on the silver-eyed one."

"And who might you be?" Birlerion asked.

"You don't need to know."

Birlerion laughed. "Not proud of what you're doing, is that it?"

"Bring him," the Kirshan leader said and stomped off.

Birlerion bent over Versillion and whispered, "Help is coming, brother. Hold on." He gripped Versillion's shoulder before he was dragged away.

Ari arrived as Birlerion was convulsed in a coughing fit. The Kirshan camp was no more than rugs on the sand, no shelter to speak of. Birlerion's hands were tied behind his back, and the strain on his chest and the dusty atmosphere were causing him problems. He dragged in a breath and wheezed as he swayed. *"Tell Illiserille and Kayerille that Kirshans attacked Medera Maraine. She escaped to Rabat, but Versillion is injured. Only seven men alive. We are held in Koav."*

Ari blinked out.

15

Oscar leaned against the doorframe of his office, watching Kayerille in the sparring ring. She was certainly putting his men through the wringer. Sweat dripped off them. They had stripped to the waist, and their pale skin gleamed in the sunlight.

After sparring with Ashton, she called a halt. Oscar couldn't take his eyes off her. She was amazing to watch. She threw a towel at Ashton, and as he dried himself off, she rubbed a clear cream over his skin. The other men jeered at him, and he beamed.

Kayerille looked around. "Who's next?"

The men all clamoured around her.

"I meant to spar," she laughed.

"If you're going to rub that stuff on us, then sparring is no problem," one of the men said.

"It protects your skin against burning," Kayerille said.

"I think they can manage on their own," Oscar said from the edge of the ring.

"Awww, sir." The men parted.

Kayerille grinned and threw the pot at Oscar. "You need

to get a supply. These delicate flowers of yours will burn in no time. They are already turning pink, and you will too."

The men protested her description of them.

"I will add it to the list," said Oscar. "In the meantime, men, you can do each other's backs. I'm sure Kayerille has better things to do. If you don't want this"—he waved the pot in the air before throwing it to Ashton—"then you need to stay covered up."

The men scowled at him, but they broke into groups and began slapping on the grease.

Oscar nodded at Kayerille and returned to his office.

She watched him retreat before turning back to the ring.

Much later in the day, Kayerille hovered in his doorway. She leaned against his door and pulled out the stopper on her canteen and took a long pull. Wiping her mouth, she idly inspected Oscar, still seated behind his desk. He frowned at her.

"What's the matter?" she asked, pushing herself off the door and entering his office.

"Who said anything was the matter?" Oscar asked, leaning back in his chair. He threw his quill on his desk, glad for the interruption.

"You haven't stopped glaring at me since Birlerion left."

"That's not true."

"I can assure you it is. So, I ask again, what's the matter?"

Oscar flushed, and Kayerille dropped into the chair opposite him.

"I didn't want to get between you and Birlerion. It's obvious you are very close," Oscar said after a long pause.

Kayerille huffed. "He is like my brother, and he looks out

for me. He's all the family I have left. My only link to the past."

"He seems to collect family wherever he goes."

"That's because he cares. He may not be a Terolian, but he acts like one. Family is extremely important to us, and protecting each other comes first. Birlerion does it naturally."

"Fortunate for him, then."

Kayerille tilted her head. "Would you not protect your family?"

"Of course I would, but … he is not truly your brother."

"Yes, he is. He is a son of the Atolea. I am a daughter. We are family. But even before that he became family, he saved my life and the lives of my brother and sisters. It wasn't just Janis who made him family; it's just who he is."

"I don't understand."

Kayerille sighed. "Got anything stronger than water?" she asked, shaking her canteen.

Oscar rose and found a bottle and two glasses as Kayerille continued speaking.

"My family lived in Mistra. My parents, my brother Daniel, and my sisters, Lily and Mattie." She smiled wistfully. "Mattie was just a babe, not even walking yet, but we got by. My father worked all over the city; he did odd jobs, repairs, fixing stuff. He was always tinkering; he liked to know how things worked, so he was good at repairing them. Lily was the same. Many a night, the two of them would pull something apart by candlelight and put it back together."

"What about you? What did you like doing?" Oscar asked, placing the glass beside her.

Kayerille stared at the golden liquid. "I never really got the chance to find out. When I was fifteen, my father went missing. My mother took up the burden of work, cleaning and washing for others, and I cared for the children." She swirled the glass. "We survived for a while, but then my mother kept falling ill. She would recover and then have a relapse, so we swapped places." After taking a sip, she carefully placed the glass back down.

"When I was sixteen, I went to look for my father. I heard rumours about these men who were collecting people. Offering good money for a day's labour. So, I went to listen. I'd never heard anything like it before. They weren't offering work; they were demanding that people sacrifice themselves for their cause, for nothing in return, and you know what?" Kayerille lifted her head, her silver eyes flashing. "They were all falling for it. They queued up and followed those men out of town without even going home to explain where they were going. I joined the queue. My father must have done the same."

"What about your mother? How could you do that to her, especially after losing your father?"

"I told her there were men offering work and I was going to find out if that was where father went. I told her and Lily. Lily took my job; she was twelve. Well, as I expect you've guessed, I ended up in the Telusion mines."

Oscar hissed.

Kayerille shrugged, her eyes distant. "I was lucky. I survived. Many didn't. As the labour was all free, they didn't feel the need to care for us. After all, they could just go to another town and collect those foolish enough to listen."

"Did you find your father?"

"No. I searched for nearly a year. And then Birlerion came."

"On his own?" Oscar asked with surprise.

"He was travelling with Adilion and an Atolean patrol. I found out afterwards that the Ascendants had attacked them using the crystals we had mined. Killed many, injured the others. Birlerion was the only one able to ride. Instead of riding for help, he went to the mountains to find the source of the Ascendants' power to prevent them from killing the rest of his patrol.

"Anyway, I was getting ready to overpower one of the guards when a dagger thumped at my feet, and then a second, out of nowhere. I had no idea where they came from but I sat on them before anyone noticed, and then the sentry watching above fell from the gallery. Whilst the guard in front of me was distracted, I slit his throat. We managed to find the keys and escape." Kayerille paused and took another sip of her wine, savouring the flavour. "This is nice."

Oscar topped it off. "And that was Birlerion?"

"He was still Birler then," Kayerille corrected. "None of us had turned Sentinal yet. He was a Lady's Ranger, though. When I first saw him, I thought he was Terolian. Until I saw his eyes, of course, a beautiful deep blue. No Terolian had blue eyes back then.

"He recognised me, knew my name; he had been searching for me. He promised Lily he would try and find me."

"And how did he meet your sister?"

"I believe the Lady led him there. My mother had died, and the children were alone. Birler rescued them, took them to the Atolea, and asked one of the Atolean aunts to care for them. Lily asked Birlerion to find me, and he did. I showed him where the crystal cavern was." Kayerille scowled. "There were hundreds of crystal rods laid out in a pattern on the floor. In the centre was a black crystal; it was the focal point, concentrating all the power from the surrounding crystals. Birlerion told me to steal it whilst he caused a distraction."

"He's good at those," Oscar murmured.

Kayerille flashed him a smile. "By removing the central crystal, the foci, it would prevent the Ascendants from attacking Birlerion's patrol again. He had his bow with him, he managed to draw the guard's attention whilst I grabbed the crystal. We nearly succeeded and were running out of the cavern when an Ascendant challenged him. He knew Birler. Birler took the crystal and taunted the Ascendant with it."

"Why would he do that?" Oscar gasped.

"So they would chase him and not the rest of us. They were desperate to get the crystal back. We had neutralised their power. It worked. They chased him and not us, and we managed to escape towards Melila, where the Atolea found us. That was the first time I met Birlerion."

Oscar exhaled. "Quite a meeting. Not surprising he made such an impression."

"I didn't know who he was until I met Tiv'erna. I was looking for my brother and sisters when I stumbled across him in the healerie. Tiv'erna had been injured in the attack. Broke a few ribs and his leg.

"I kept him company. We got to know each other, and he told me about Birler and why he had lent him his Darian." Kayerille dipped her head. "We found much to like in each other. He later asked me to join with him."

Oscar froze. "And did you?"

"I asked him to wait," Kayerille said with difficulty. "I had just turned Sentinal, I was only seventeen and I knew I had to concentrate on the Lady's needs first. He understood. He agreed to wait."

There was an extended pause. Oscar didn't know what to say.

Kayerille suddenly looked up. "Were you jealous of Birlerion? You were, weren't you?"

Oscar felt heat rise across his face, and Kayerille laughed bitterly. "You were jealous of the wrong man. That night you interrupted us in the Atolean camp, Birlerion was telling me I had every right to a life, that Tiv'erna would be cheering me on. As Birlerion says, they are in the past, not loved less but lost all the same." Her face softened in memory.

"Kayerille, I'm so sorry. I'm an idiot."

"True, though I think it's probably Birlerion you owe an apology to."

"I suppose I do, but I owe you an apology, too. I made an assumption, and that's unforgivable, especially as I have no right to judge."

"Does this mean you'll stop glaring at me?"

Oscar grinned as he leaned over, picked up the greasy jar on his desk, and hefted it in hand. "Only if you rub some of this stuff on my back."

"What time are you off duty?" she asked with a grin. Suddenly, she stiffened. "Someone just arrived via the waystone."

Oscar stared at her. "Were you expecting anyone?"

"No, though they should have reached Marmera by now. Maybe it is Virenion with word."

16

Kayerille and Oscar were waiting when Virenion strode into the garrison. His silver eyes and shimmering robes gained him entrance, and his rather dour face lightened as he saw Kayerille. "Birlerion said you would be here."

"They reached Marmera safely, then," she replied as they hugged.

"Yes, they didn't stop but left for Rabat. I warned Illiserille to expect them. Birlerion suggested I call in and meet Commander Landis."

"Then please join us. We were going to relax with a cool drink. The days seem to be getting hotter," Oscar said as he led the way to the open arbour.

"If you can survive the next two months, you can survive anything," Virenion said with a grin.

"When I get the chance, I will visit Marmera and the outlying districts, but I think I'll wait for the cooler season."

"Don't blame you. Though, once you've seen one part of the desert, it is all much the same."

"Virenion, how can you! Terolia is not all desert and has many beauties."

Oscar chuckled at Kayerille's passionate defence of her homeland.

Virenion grinned. "Of which you are one, but sand is sand wherever you are."

"Oh, you. Are you staying for dinner?"

"If you'll have me. Birlerion is right. We should visit more often."

"How was he?"

"He looked fine to me. Why wouldn't he be?"

"He is still recovering from Oprimere. He is not fully fit yet."

"Well, you wouldn't know by looking at him. He was the one insisting they kept moving." Virenion turned his attention to Oscar. "Commander Landis, what do you think of Terolia so far?"

"It has been very welcoming. I think I will like it here."

"I must admit, I was surprised when Birlerion said you had set up here. Weren't there more suitable locations?"

"Like where?"

"Well, Marmera is more central, or even Rabat."

"I think this is a good starting point, though, of course, we are here as the king's representatives for all of Terolia, not just Mistra."

"Good luck with that. I expect most folks will think you are just here to protect Mistra."

Oscar frowned. "How do we stop that?"

"Spread the word, I suppose. You need to meet all the Families, not just the Atolea."

"Maybe you should have gone with Birlerion and the Medera," Kayerille said thoughtfully.

"I'm beginning to think I should have."

"Virenion can take you through the waystone, if you like."

"I have Viktor to worry about."

Kayerille smiled mischievously. "We could bring him, too. Only Birlerion is not allowed to use them."

"I'm sure Viktor would love that," Oscar said, rolling his eyes.

"Aww, come on, commander. Live a bit. What's a little bit of nausea in the scheme of things?"

"A little bit would be ok, but that's not what you are selling."

Virenion laughed. "Kayerille, I don't think he's buying."

"Worth a try," she said, sinking into the cushions. "We were going to join Viktor for dinner. I'm sure you would be welcome, too."

"I stopped on the way here and spoke to him. He is expecting us."

"How efficient of you. What news is there?"

Oscar watched as Kayerille skilfully extracted all she wanted to know from Virenion. From the gleam in Virenion's eye, he was sure this was a game they both liked to play.

As the sun dipped behind the buildings, they strolled through the peaceful streets to the Atolean camp. Children's voices carried on the air, happy and carefree. Torches and lanterns were lit, offering pools of golden light to lead the way. Oscar smiled as they entered the tent, bowing with hands clasped in response to Viktor's welcome.

"You've met our eldest daughter, haven't you? This is Elis'ande."

An elegant young woman bowed. "Lady's greetings," she said, her voice light and smooth.

They relaxed into the welcome, and Viktor patted the cushions next to him. "Commander Oscar, join me."

Once Oscar had sat down, Viktor peered at him. "How are you settling in?"

"Fine, thank you. Kayerille has been helping us acclimatise," Oscar replied as he watched the two young women talk.

"Excellent. She needs something to keep her busy. She is on her own here much of the time. Your garrison will be just what she needs. Our Sentinals need help adjusting to the new Remargaren. We wouldn't want to lose them through lack of vigilance."

Oscar frowned. "I don't understand."

"The Sentinals come from a different age. They have accepted us without complaint. But don't you think they might miss what they have lost?"

"I suppose," Oscar said. "I hadn't considered it."

Viktor tried a different tack. "How well do you know Birlerion?"

"Not very well, I suppose I know more of him. He was always with Commander Haven, achieving the impossible."

"Yes, he does that. He always seems to find himself in the middle of trouble, even now. I suppose it is because he is so competent that everyone relies on him." Viktor peered at Oscar. "Who can Birlerion rely on?"

"What do you mean?"

"Well, when you think of Birlerion, who is backing him up?"

Oscar faltered. "I don't know. Versillion?"

"Versillion is normally in Greens. His duty is there. He told me he is only here because Birlerion insisted on coming to find his Darian and Versillion knew he wouldn't make it on his own. There is no one behind Birlerion because he is the protector; he protects the Lady's captain. So, he relies on whatever family is around him at the time; the Sentinals, Greens, and the Descelles, us. But none of us is truly his family. His family died three thousand years ago; the Greens, the Atoleans, they are all dead."

"He has his brothers and Marianille."

"True, and how often are they together? He feels alone, as does Kayerille and all the other Sentinals. They struggle to adjust. It's been just over a year since they were awoken, and they are still adjusting. You need to give them time. They only have each other. They are the only thing that is familiar in this strange new world. Don't vilify them for that."

Oscar flushed. "I don't mean to."

"This is why his Darian is so important. The relationship between a man and a Darian is almost indescribable; you are linked to another being who is attuned to your every thought. Losing that link is like a part of you dying, and you must remember, Birlerion lost his first Darian. I can't imagine what he must have gone through when he first awoke. Lesser men would have been incapacitated."

"I didn't know he had a Darian. Before, I mean."

"He doesn't mention it. I doubt many people know. Tomorrow, I'll introduce you to mine, give you a taste of what we're talking about. It might help you understand. A Darian is a gift from the Lady, one to be honoured and treasured."

"They are rare outside of Terolia, aren't they?"

"Very rare. Family comes in many shapes and sizes. The fear of losing it again can be paralysing. It takes courage to start a new one," Viktor said as Per'serre helped him rise. "I look forward to continuing our conversation another time. But now, I think our dinner is ready."

They were interrupted as Kayerille and Virenion lurched to their feet, staring wildly at the air in front of them. Kayerille extended her hands. "Where? Where were they attacked?"

"Outside Koav. That is Koav he is showing us," Virenion hissed.

Oscar scowled at them. "What are you talking about? Who is showing you?"

The air shimmered, and an airborne creature appeared in front of Oscar, a bundle of brown and black fur hovering under scaly grey wings. The creature chittered, and Oscar was bombarded by a cascade of visons, ending with Birlerion kneeling in the sand, his arms tied behind his back.

"The Medera's party has been attacked," Oscar gasped.

Viktor's voice cracked as he asked. "What about Maraine?"

"She's no longer with Birlerion." Kayerille paled. "Only seven men remain."

Ari chittered.

"He says Rabat. Maraine headed for Rabat," Kayerille said.

"Then that is where we need to go. We must meet her there. Can you take us?" Viktor asked.

"Of course, but Sodera, the effects of travelling by waystone are terrible. Are you sure?" Kayerille asked.

"I could take some men to Marmera and approach Koav from the south," Virenion offered.

"Of course I'm sure," Viktor snapped. "Per'serre, get some men ready to go with Virenion. We'll go with Kayerille."

"Virenion, can you check with Illiserille in Rabat first?" asked Oscar. "Make sure Viktor isn't walking into another trap? See if there is any word of Maraine."

"Good idea. I won't be long." Virenion rushed out of the tent.

"Viktor, I recommend you move your camp to Marmera tomorrow," said Oscar. "At least your family will be closer to help if needed. It sounds like Maraine's patrol has been decimated. Until we know what has happened, I suggest we get as many men in the vicinity as possible."

"We should have followed Maraine to Rabat already," Viktor said, his face pale.

"My men will accompany you. This is what we are here for."

"Oscar, the transition through the waystone will leave your men helpless when they come out the other end," Kayerille warned.

"Then we'd better arrive in the dark. I will go and mobilise them. I'll meet you back here."

17

Someone kicking his legs jerked Birlerion awake. His coughing fit had exhausted him and he had dozed off. He inhaled the scent of baked sands, still warm after being burned by the sun all day, and he started coughing again. He rolled over and sat up, trying to breathe as his chest spasmed. The bindings on his arms strained his chest muscles. He folded inwards as much as possible as he concentrated on inhaling air. A fire had been lit, and the aroma of kafinee drifted on the evening air.

"You said you were at the conclave." A wiry young Kirshan warrior sat opposite him. The flickering flames of the fire glinted in his gleaming black eyes. He had removed his scarves, and his black hair straggled limply around his face. His face was covered by a close-clipped beard that didn't disguise his firm jaw. This was not the man who had attacked him earlier.

"Yes."

"Tell me what happened."

Birlerion tilted his head and breathed carefully. "You don't know?"

"I want the truth."

"Do you know why the conclave was called?"

The man hesitated. "No," he admitted, looking down at his kafinee.

Birlerion closed his eyes. Where to start? "Any chance of some water?"

The man jerked his head, and the Kirshan guard behind him uncapped his canteen and helped Birlerion drink.

After taking another careful breath, Birlerion began. "The Ascendants tried to destroy the Families, having already attempted to overthrow King Benedict. They culled people from Eastern Terolia and forced them to work in the mines that they'd dug in the Falusion mountains." He stopped to cough, and the Kirshan frowned. "For over three years, they worked people to death—men, women, and children—for no reason; just because they could. Families were wiped out and villages emptied, and the Mederas didn't know."

"What's wrong with you?" the Kirshan asked as Birlerion stopped to cough again. His chest wheezed.

"Sand in my throat," Birlerion choked, and the guard offered him some more water. Birlerion struggled on, his voice edged with a rasp.

"It all came to light when Captain Haven traced the Ascendants to Mistra and then to the Telusions, what you now call the Falusion Mountains. When he arrived, the Ascendants had already left, leaving over a thousand people to die in that mountain." Birlerion's face hardened. "They blew the mountain up. We managed to save forty-two. The Lady demanded the Medera's meet in conclave. When the facts were presented, the Mederas made excuses. The Captain had to remind them of Family Law."

The Kirshan choked. "That's not possible. The Mederas remember all."

Birlerion glanced across the fire at him. "I wondered if

the Kirshans still followed Family Law or had discarded it completely."

"You know nothing of Family Law."

"I know more than you think. Anyway, the Captain asked each Family to swear to the Lady and uphold Family Law, with the intent that the Families would continue to manage internal rule according to Family Law. In return, King Benedict would offer protection to all. Kirsha was the only family that refused." Birlerion stopped speaking to drag in a breath.

"You lie," a new voice said from behind Birlerion, the voice harsh and cold.

"Unfortunately, Medera Silva had succumbed to an Ascendant mind spell. They offered her superiority over all families, and in return, she would assist them in their endeavours. She created a network for the Ascendants to move goods and people." Birlerion paused to take breath and clear the huskiness in his voice. The man closed in behind him and he held still, aware of the threat hovering over him.

"That is not true. Kirshans do not submit to others."

"I suggest you check the routes that supply Port Feril. I think you'll find they are not as legitimate as you think. Haven't you spoken to your own people?"

A sudden movement behind Birlerion made him turn, and a man struck him, and Birlerion collapsed into the sand, dazed. He twisted, trying to keep the sand out of his face. His breath rattled in his chest as he shifted awkwardly, and the strain on his chest made him gasp for air.

"Sir'elo! That was not necessary." The Kirshan warrior leapt to his feet.

"Stop listening to him; he twists the truth. You can't trust the betrayers."

"He was there; his words are true."

"Yer'ota, be very careful. Medera Silva will be reinstated.

She is the lawful Medera of Kirsha. Outsiders do not have the right to dictate Family rule."

Yer'ota clamped his mouth shut.

Birlerion tried not to cough and failed.

"Kill him," Sir'elo ordered.

"What?"

"He's a betrayer. Kill him."

"He is a Lady's Sentinal. We can't kill him."

There was a short silence. "Are you questioning me, Yer'ota?"

"Of course not."

"Then kill him now."

"Sir'elo, please. We can't betray the Lady."

"She's not here. She doesn't care about Kirsha. Kill him."

"Leyandrii does care. She protected your people when you didn't," Birlerion croaked.

Sir'elo grabbed Birlerion's hair and pulled him back up onto his knees, exposing his throat. "My mother protects our people, not you."

"Threatening to kill Medera Maraine will not reinstate Kirsha," Birlerion gasped.

"Stop talking. Kill him, Yer'ota."

"Why don't *you* do it? Afraid to cross the Lady yourself?" Birlerion jeered. He inhaled as Sir'elo bent him back. Bitter black eyes met his as cold steel rested against his throat.

"Say your goodbyes."

Val'eria's cry warned him that Versillion had tried to rise.

Birlerion threw his thoughts across the desert. *"Kin'arol? I am so sorry."* His panicked farewell sparked an immediate response.

"Birlerion? No! You are mine! Rigs, stop them." Kin'arol's fear surged through him, dispelling his regrets.

The tableau was broken as a horse screamed and

charged across the campsite. A blur of brown muscle ploughed into Sir'elo and Birlerion. Birlerion spun around, stunned and off balance. Yer'ota caught him and dragged him away from the fire.

Birlerion regained consciousness to find Val'eria hovering over him. It was pitch black, the shadows relieved by the fire, which had been built up and now had a larger pot hanging over it. "Take it easy, Birlerion. You took quite a blow."

Yer'ota stood behind her. "Birlerion?"

Val'eria flushed. "Yes, he is Birlerion. The other is Versillion. I didn't think you would let him live if I had told you the truth."

Yer'ota's face pinched, and he walked away.

Birlerion groaned and sat up, sending sand showering around him. He felt pummelled; his shoulder and chest ached. He realised his hands were free, and he felt his neck; the sting of the knife's edge was still vivid. The wound was bandaged. "What happened? How come they released us?"

"As I understand it, a horse went beserk and ran you down. You didn't manage to get out of the way quickly enough. The Kirshan is dead," Val'eria reported, holding him steady. "Yer'ota took it as a sign from the Lady and ordered everyone released. We agreed to help each other as none of us were fit to move on."

"Is the Darian alright?"

"Yes, he is fine. Drink this."

"Good." Birlerion closed his eyes as he swallowed the draught. *"Kin'arol, what did you do?"*

"I come."

A horse of few words. It seemed his Darian was an independent spirit.

"*Where are you?*"

"*I come. Stay there.*"

"*Who is Rigs?*"

"*She helped me escape.*" A brief image of a petite but scruffy child flashed through Birlerion's mind. "*She can speak to Darian's. She spoke to one in your camp.*"

"*So that's why the bay went beserk,*" Birlerion thought, glad to have it explained. "*Be careful and look after her.*"

"*Of course!*"

Birlerion had to grin at his Darian's affronted tone. He lay back down with a groan, at least his chest didn't feel so tight. "How is Versillion?" he asked Val'eria.

"Awake and worried about you."

"Then we'd better go and reassure him. What about the other men?"

"Cuts and bruises. Nothing serious."

"And the Terolians?"

"Likewise, though we have eleven fatalities and they have fifteen."

Twenty-six men dead. Birlerion's stomach roiled as he stood. He tottered over to Versillion, who was lying under a makeshift awning. Val'eria followed and crouched next to Versillion.

"How did you manage to break a leg?" Birlerion asked.

Versillion scowled at him. "How did you manage to tame the Kirshans?"

Birlerion rubbed his neck. "I didn't think I had."

Val'eria slapped his hand away. "Leave it alone. Versillion, you need to drink more water. Birlerion, tell him."

"You need to drink more water," Birlerion repeated, "or you'll be upsetting the lovely healer."

Val'eria glared at him, and Birlerion meekly raised his brother's shoulders. Val'eria tilted the canteen against Versillion's lips. "I am not completely helpless," Versillion growled.

Birlerion chuckled. "Make the most of it. The ride home is going to be long and painful."

"Don't." Versillion groaned as he closed his eyes against the thought.

"He won't be going anywhere for a while," said Val'eria. "His leg needs to start mending before we can move him."

"And there are no waystones nearby," Birlerion said with a grimace.

"You can't use them, anyway," Versillion said.

"It must be three months since Oprimere by now."

Versillion shifted uncomfortably, his face strained. "You'll wait until the healers clear you. Don't argue, Birlerion."

Clenching his jaw, Birlerion nodded to appease his brother. "Rest, Versillion. None of us are going anywhere right now."

Val'eria stoppered the canteen and rose. "Birlerion, you need to speak to the Kirshans. We need to rig a proper shelter, and we need blankets for tonight."

Birlerion left the healer fussing over his brother and scanned the campsite. Yer'ota was inspecting his men. Birlerion stopped a short distance away. "Yer'ota, we need to talk."

The Terolian looked up and stared at Birlerion. One of the men muttered beside him, and Yer'ota stiffened. The man spoke again, and Yer'ota bent to help him stand. He was older, greying at the temples and thicker around the waist, but the family resemblance was startling. Birlerion waited.

"I am Yer'ana, father of Yer'ota, cousin of Silva."

"Birlerion, son of the Atolea."

"We would leave you in peace, but we have wounded men who can't be moved. Sir'elo, son of Silva, has paid the price for his mistake. The Lady has spoken, and we listen."

"We are in no fit state to move ourselves. It will be

simpler to build one camp, we have few supplies between us." Birlerion observed the Kirshans. None would meet his eyes, they seemed embarrassed, dejected even, as if someone had berated them for their behaviour, no sign of Sir'elo's belligerence. He took a leap of faith. "I suggest we join forces and build a shelter for all our wounded. That would make it easier for our healer to treat them. We also need to recover those who fell."

Yer'ana bowed, clasping his hands against his chest. "Your forbearance is appreciated. Yer'ota will assist you." Yer'ota helped him sit back in the sand; his father's face was pale and dewed with sweat from the effort.

Birlerion strode over to the remains of the tent the Atolea had been raising when they were attacked and began gathering poles. The walking wounded stood to help him. "We need to build the shelter over the Kirshan wounded. They have some men who can't be moved." He paused by Val'eria. "What is wrong with the elderly Kirshan?"

"Elderly? I haven't treated any elderly men, only youngsters."

"Yer'ota's father is wounded. Come with me." Birlerion crouched beside the older man. "Wounds should not be allowed to fester in the desert heat."

Strained black eyes inspected him. "I'm fine."

"No, you aren't. Let Val'eria help you."

Yer'ana closed his eyes. "We betrayed the Lady, attacked her people. We are not worthy of her attention."

"We are all worthy of her attention. She doesn't give up on you as easily as you gave up on her. Maybe that is a lesson you can learn from all of this."

"I think we have many lessons to learn," Yer'ana breathed, but he didn't protest when Val'eria tugged open his robes. Birlerion left her to her work and went to help the men raise the makeshift awning.

A second shelter was raised over the horses, picketed next to them. Birlerion stroked the bay Darian who had charged them. His rich brown coat gleamed in the torchlight. *"Thank you for your assistance. It was timely,"* he thought, rubbing the Darian's nose. *"I'm sorry I have no baliweed to thank you with, but when I do, you'll be first in line."*

The bay whickered and rubbed his head against Birlerion's chest.

"He's yours," Yer'ota said from behind him.

Birlerion's hand stilled. "I already have a Darian, and this fine fellow will need time to mourn before anyone else claims him."

Yer'ota moved around to the other side of the bay and stroked his neck. He met Birlerion's eyes. "For a Vespirian, you understand much that you should not know."

"There is much I do not understand, but the sands always welcome me."

"So they should, son of the Atolea. I wish we had met before Sir'elo led us all astray. It would have been clear that this was not the Lady's desire."

"Has no other stepped forward to replace Silva? Kirsha has a place at the table if you can choose another. Silva chose greed over family. She will never be accepted by the conclave; there must be another."

"Would you come and speak before the Family? I will guarantee your safety. The Family does not understand what happened. They need to be told the truth; otherwise, we will never be able to move forward. They will not choose another whilst they believe Silva has the right to lead us."

"What of Silva? Why does she still preside? The conclave removed her authority."

Yer'ota squinted into the distance. "I think our time will be spent unravelling the lies she told. My Family doesn't know what to believe and, as such, remains incapacitated, no doubt by design. Her son, Sir'elo, was her front, eager to maintain her position and his. I don't believe her daughter, Riv'ella, could have known. She would never have walked away from the Lady. I can't believe she would do such a thing."

"You did not walk away from the Lady, Yer'ota. You were misled. It can be difficult to make the right decisions when you are fed lies."

"But still, we should have challenged them."

"I think the other Families should have been clearer about what happened. Everyone in Terolia should under-stand why your leaders chose to give their allegiance to King Benedict. It was not a decision made lightly."

"You have to explain it, Birlerion, please. How can my Family decide if we are mired in untruths?"

"The Atolea may have a prior claim on your time. You did attack Medera Maraine. She is not happy, nor will her Sodera be when he finds out."

"She *was* with you!"

"Oh, yes."

Yer'ota rubbed his eyes. "I suppose we deserve all we get. Sir'elo is the lucky one; he has already paid his price and leaves the rest of us to pay the balance."

Birlerion surveyed the rough-and-ready camp. "I think you have already paid."

"No, we haven't."

"That will be for the Medera to decide when she arrives. Which I expect she will tomorrow. But I promise, if, after the Medera has spoken, you still want me to explain to your Family what really happened all those months ago, I'll do it."

"Good. Until then, come with me. We have food and coffee. Join us. I am quite sure tomorrow will be a difficult day."

18

Oscar heaved the contents of his guts all over the sand. "What I do for you," he groaned as he collapsed outside the waystone in Rabat.

Kayerille's eyes sparkled. "For me?"

"For you Sentinals," Oscar corrected between heaves. Kayerille smiled as she rubbed his back and offered him the canteen of water. His men fared no better. Per'serre hovered over Viktor; neither were particularly happy.

The horses milled around their riders, watching them with bemused expressions.

"I'm not doing that again … I don't care how fast it is. My guts feel like they've been ripped out," a young private said between retches as he knelt in the silver sands. The moon glistened in the clear night sky, revealing their distress in all its uncomfortable glory.

"I did warn you," Kayerille said.

"Mere words," Oscar whispered, his throat burning, "are nothing to the reality."

She chuckled as Illiserille arrived.

"Ah," Illiserille said, surveying the men. She hurried to offer more water. Her lips twitched as she returned to Kayerille's side. "I suppose there is no point offering them a tagine for dinner."

Oscar turned away and heaved again.

"Don't be so mean," Kayerille replied, trying not to laugh.

"They will need food in their stomachs before you go. I assume you intend to leave for Koav as soon as they are able? Virenion told me that much before he left. Is there any further word of Birlerion and Versillion?"

"No, nothing. What about Medera Maraine? Has she arrived?" Kayerille asked.

"Not yet, but Medera Reina is camped to the north. I have told her what we know, and she has sent some of her men to go and scout," Illiserille said.

"I'll escort Sodera Viktor to the Solari camp if you would keep an eye on Oscar and his men for me," Kayerille suggested.

Casting an eye over the men, Illiserille grimaced. "Meet us back at my place. The walk will do them good, give them something else to think about."

Kayerille left to collect Viktor, who appeared to be in better shape than his men. Per'serre had assisted him back into his saddle, and as Viktor smiled down at her, the moon's shine made a halo of his grey turban. "Well, that wasn't so bad, was it?"

"Speak for yourself," Per'serre said as he pulled his horse near. He rested his head against the saddle before, with a grunt of effort, launching himself up. He swallowed and gripped the pommel before shifting uncomfortably.

"Maybe the Darian helps mitigate the effects of the waystone. We'll have to experiment when we have time. For now, let's get you to the Solari camp. Maraine should be arriving soon," Kayerille said. Mounting her horse, she led the way as Viktor and Per'serre followed.

The first to arrive in Koav were the Solari advance patrols, precursors to the arrival of Medera Reina. They approached the camp cautiously, circling the makeshift awnings as dawn spread out over the golden sands. Birlerion strode out to meet them. After a quick discussion, they followed him into the camp, sending one man to report to the Medera.

Birlerion blessed Medera Reina for listening and being prepared to meet them in Rabat. Although Rabat was still a good day's ride away, he didn't expect any further help to arrive for another day at the earliest. According to the Solari patrol leader, the Kirshans were nowhere to be seen, and Yer'ota grew tenser as time passed.

The Solari found the camp peaceful but busy. They helped move the dead into the caves, out of the heat, and haggled for more canvas to wrap them in from the villagers. Stray horses were collected, their injuries were treated, and the camp was slowly put to rights as the three Families pulled together.

"Who'd have thought you would be working side by side with those you thought were your enemies?" Birlerion said to Yer'ota as they paused in their grisly work of slowly sewing the canvas shrouds.

Yer'ota wiped his arm over his forehead. It was swelter-ing. "The Lady works to show us humility," he said, twisting his lips.

"Not necessarily. You could have delegated this to someone else."

"As could you."

"True."

Leaning back on his heels, Yer'ota peered at Birlerion. "Tell me the truth. You knew the Lady? You walked in her shadow?"

"Oh, yes. I knelt at her feet, held her when she cried, and felt the lash of her tongue when she was angry." Birlerion paused. "And I have been blessed with her love and protection since I was a child." He laughed self-consciously. "And no doubt, I've caused her many headaches, but her regard never falters, nor does my devotion to her. It may have been over three thousand years, but to me, it is as if it was yesterday, and if I turn around, she'll be standing there, waiting for me to return from whatever errand she sent me on. After all, we are here on her behalf to protect those who cannot protect themselves."

"Do you think she sent you here deliberately? To help us?"

Birlerion stilled. "I wouldn't put it past her, but if she did, she chose the most convoluted way."

"I expect we managed to mess up her plans. I am sure she would have avoided all this if she could."

"Indeed, she can only work with the tools she has, and that's us, I'm afraid. We don't always do what she wants us to, no matter how hard she tries."

They fell silent and returned to their sewing. The air cooled imperceptibly, and Birlerion smiled.

The next to arrive were the Kirshans. The Solaris tensed as the caravan arrived. Birlerion watched Yer'ota approach the lead wagon and speak briefly with its driver before moving further down the line.

The driver whipped his horses up and began circling the wagon. The others followed, their colourful wagons filled with uncertainty and suspicion. Yer'ota was soon surrounded by gesticulating men. As their voices rose in anger, Birlerion moved closer.

"Birlerion, wait. Where are you going?" One of the Solarian warriors tried to pull him back, but Birlerion shrugged him off.

A wiry man dressed in baggy trousers and a long-sleeved shirt stood before Yer'ota. "We need to wipe these betrayers from our lands. Yer'ota, what do you think you are doing, allowing them to live?" His face was taut with anger. "You say they killed our children, yet you aid them?"

"In self-defence, uncle; we attacked them. They aid us, if truth be told."

"You surrendered to the betrayers?" the man gasped. "You embarrass us with your failure, and you will pay the price."

"No, he won't," Birlerion said, striding up beside Yer'ota.

An elderly man with bowed shoulders stepped forward. "Who do you think you are, speaking for the Medera?"

"He speaks for the Lady. Can't you see?" Yer'ota said.

"You've been out in the sun too long. Your wits are addled." The wiry man turned away. "He wastes our time."

"Sar'iva, uncle, please listen." Yer'ota grasped the wiry man's arm, but he shook him off.

"It's time the Kirshans stopped arguing and listened," Birlerion said. "Silva leads you away from the Lady's path. Don't you want to know why?"

A ripple of murmurs spread through the listening crowd, and Yer'ota stepped forward. "Convene the Family. Let him speak. He was in Mistra when the Mederas met. Hear the truth of what happened."

"You dare call our Medera a liar?" Sar'iva spat.

"Silva is no longer the voice of Kirsha. It is time for you to choose a new Medera who can lead you out of this spiral of self-destruction," Birlerion said, raising his voice over the angry exclamations.

A young woman with the smooth bronze skin of youth

stepped forward, lithe and straight. Her stern face was framed by sleek black hair pulled into a plait which was held in place by a wide orange bandana. "Enough!" Her voice was sharp and commanding. "What is this commotion?"

"Riv'ella, Sir'elo is dead. What shall we tell the Medera?" Sar'iva said in the sudden silence.

"Yer'ota calls the Medera a liar and says we should listen to a betrayer," a rounder version of Sar'iva said.

Riv'ella frowned at them. "Yer'ota, speak plain. What has happened?"

"Would it not be simpler to explain this to all in conclave once instead of repeating it piecemeal?" Birlerion suggested, keeping his voice calm.

Riv'ella's glance flensed him. "And you are?"

"This is Sentinal Birlerion of the Lady's Guard," Yer'ota said. "Birlerion, this is Riv'ella, daughter of Silva, sister of Sir'elo."

"The silver-eyed ones were the betrayers of Terolia. They caused the rift within the Families. They are no Lady's Guard. Take him," Sar'ila urged.

Yer'ota stood in front of Birlerion. "No one harms him."

Riv'ella scowled at him. "Why would you stand with our enemy? Yer'ota, you stand against your Family."

"Riv'ella, our mother is ill, misled. She leads us astray and charges us to do terrible deeds. If we are to survive as a Family, we need to listen to what he has to say."

"No, you are the one who has been misled."

Yer'ota gritted his teeth. "What will it take to get you all to listen?" he snapped. "If we continue in this manner, we will regret it. Attacking other Families, losing sons for no reason. Why? Why are we fighting? Because the Medera decrees it. She is twisted and lost, but that doesn't mean we have to be lost, too."

"Be very careful, Yer'ota. My brother always said you

were a steady warrior. Do not jeopardise your place in the Family," Riv'ella said, her voice sharp.

"There will be no Family if you don't listen to me. I followed Sir'elo like a lamb, questioning nothing, and where did he take us? He brought us here." Yer'ota threw out his arm. "To attack Medera Maraine as she travelled to meet Medera Reina."

Riv'ella's face blanched. "He did what?"

"He did what I told him to, like any good son should. Where is he? Where is my Sir'elo?" A tall woman pushed her way through the crowd, fingers gripping like claws on Yer'ota's shoulder. Her face was lined and wrinkled, her brown skin faded and aged before her time. Strands of greyish brown hair escaped the severe coils plaited on her head, and her beady black eyes darted around her.

"Mother, did you order Sir'elo to attack the Atolean Medera?" Riv'ella asked.

"Yes." The woman smiled at the familiar faces. Her gaze reached Birlerion, and she made a guttural snarl, deep in her throat. She bared her teeth, her eyes wide and enraged, and then she shrieked, "Kill him! Kill him now before he destroys us!" She twisted around, wrenched a dagger from Sar'iva's belt, and launched herself at Birlerion.

Yer'ota batted her arm up, but she barrelled forward and Birlerion went down, trying to fend her off. It took both Yer'ota and Sar'iva to pull her off him. Spittle flew from her mouth as she screeched insults, her words meaningless as she tried to kick out at Birlerion.

The Kirshans stared in horror as their Medera collapsed in the men's arms and wept. They relaxed their grip, and she squirmed away and pounced back on top of the rising Birlerion, her bony fingers gripping his neck.

Birlerion struggled to breathe. As she crushed his windpipe, black and gold sparks appeared before his eyes, and he fumbled for his dagger, barely aware of the commotion going on around him. Men shouted, horses squealed and then the woman slumped over him, her grip loosening. She was pulled off him again. Yer'ota knelt beside him and helped him sit. "Birlerion, by the Lady, are you alright? She was so strong. I am so sorry."

Birlerion gasped for breath, coughing as the familiar tightness spread across his chest. "I'm fine," he wheezed.

Riv'ella stood over him, breathing heavily, a bloody dagger gripped in her hand. Her knuckles gleamed ivory with the strength of her grip, and she flinched away from Yer'ota's concerned gaze. "Enough!" she commanded, glaring at her fellow Kirshans. "When he is recovered, we convene. The Family will hear his words." She looked down at her mother's body and tightened her lips. "We have much to discuss."

19

A large fire burned brightly in the centre of the convene. Kirshans of all ages sat around it in the shape of a horseshoe, leaving one end open. The youngest, curled up at the feet of their elders, stared around, wide-eyed.

The injured Kirshans had been carried into the camp and reunited with their families. All were present. As Riv'ella stepped forward, the firelight burnished her skin to gold. Yer'ota sat on the end, his dark eyes following her every move.

She glanced at him briefly before beginning. "Our Family is in a time of crisis. Our beloved Medera has strayed from the path of the Lady and brought our Family name into disrepute. She ordered Kirshan sons to perform terrible acts. She and they have paid for that error with the final price, their lives. A life for a life; but our balance sheet still leaves us owing.

"Before we can begin to balance what we owe, we need to understand how we came to be here. There is one who has the knowledge, and even though I have tried many times to take his life, he is prepared to speak to us and for us.

Once we have heard his words, we will say farewell to those we have lost."

Riv'ella took a deep breath. "And then we will vote for a new Medera to lead us, to help us balance what we owe and restore our Family honour and name. We will all need to come together and support our new Medera in what will be a long and difficult task. We will need to work together as one Family." She stepped back and gestured. "Listen with your heart as well as your ears, for this is our chance to understand. The Lady is near, and she is watching; may she guide us true.

"I bring before you Sentinal Birlerion of the Lady's Guard, who lived in the time of the Lady and protected both her and her people. He is here now in our time of need. Listen well."

Birlerion stepped in front of her and into the firelight. His green robes shimmered and his silver eyes gleamed. The moonlight gilded his skin and bleached away his new bruises. He glowed in the eyes of the Kirshans, and they watched him in silence as he began to speak.

"My name is Birlerion. I became a Lady's Ranger in 1120 and a Lady's Sentinal in 1123. I was with the Lady when she sundered the Bloodstone and brought down the Veil to protect us all, and I have slept for three thousand years.

"I was awoken in what is now called Old Vespers in the year 4124. I was awoken because a new Ascendant curse threatened our world; a threat that tried to overthrow King Benedict of Vespiri, the Grand Duke of Elothia, and Terolian Family Law.

"I came to Terolia with Commander Haven. Where we travelled, we awoke new Sentinals, but we also heard rumours of lost Terolians. We travelled to Marmera and Melila, and we found history repeating itself.

"Villages were deserted and the people missing, but no one knew why. We travelled to what is now called the Falusion mountains and found what remained of them." Birlerion took a deep breath, his face hardening as he described what they had found under the mountains. His audience stirred and gasped in horror. Although he tempered his description due to the small children listening, from his omissions, the elders understood.

"We returned to Mistra, and the Lady's Captain requested that Medera Maraine call a conclave; a meeting of the leaders of all six Terolian families. In that meeting, Captain Haven told them what I have just told you.

"They made excuses for why they were too busy fighting with each other or themselves to care for their people." Birlerion looked around his avid audience. "The Captain had to remind them of Family Law. Not just Kirsha, but all the Families.

"He had to remind them why they were leaders and what the Lady expected of them. He asked them to restate the Lady's Oath and offered Terolia the protection of King Benedict and Vespiri against external threats on the condition that your leaders led their Families according to Family Law."

He paused as a low murmur began. "At no time was Family structure questioned. The Ascendants tried to destroy that, not Captain Haven nor King Benedict. The only Medera and Sodera who refused were Silva and Ricard of Kirsha."

A groan swept around the convene, and mutters of dismay grew.

"There is an Ascendant mind-control spell called *Mentiserium*. Those who don't hold the Lady close are susceptible. It gives others the power over your actions, your choices. Kirsha chose greed, succumbed to the Ascendants, and agreed to help them in return for ascendancy over all the Families.

"During the conclave in front of all the Families, Silva admitted that she had allowed the Ascendants access to the Falusion mountains and the port of Feril. She had kept suspicious eyes averted, as well as her own Family's, and drawn attention away from the region so the Ascendants could do their terrible work.

"As a result, the conclave voted to remove Silva and Ricard from their positions. They should never have been able to return and resume their leadership. This is a true rendition of what happened at the Family conclave in Mistra."

Birlerion stopped speaking and accepted a canteen of water, smiling at the small child who offered it. He took a deep swallow and waited.

Yer'ota stood forward. "Any questions?"

"How do we know he speaks true? He killed Sir'elo."

"A Darian killed Sir'elo as he attempted to take the life of this Lady's Guard. I was there. I witnessed it. Birlerion did not kill Sir'elo; the Lady's instrument did, protecting her guard."

"Why is he here? What does he want with Kirsha?" Another voice asked.

"The only reason I came to Terolia was to retrieve my Darian, who was stolen from Greens three months ago. The Atolea and Greens had an agreement dating back to when I first walked this land. The agreement was more to strengthen a bond of friendship and family. The Atolea promised to send a Darian to Greens once a generation in my memory. The Atoleans have honoured that agreement for three thousand years. This year they sent a Darian for me. But I was delayed while recovering in Oprimere, and when I was well enough to return home, he was gone, stolen."

"He is still missing," Yer'ota said, his voice low.

Riv'ella stepped up next to Yer'ota, who took a step back. "We will digest Sentinal Birlerion's words. We thank him for his honesty. We will say farewell to those we lost, and tomorrow we reconvene and vote. We will convene until a choice is made, and then the Medera will take us to Rabat, where we will return those wounded by our error."

Riv'ella extended her hand to Birlerion. "Sentinal Birlerion, I swear we will find your Darian for you and return him to you."

"Thank you."

"But for now, we have our farewells to say and difficult decisions to make. Tomorrow, if you will permit us, we will take your wounded back to their Medera."

"I will send word to Rabat. Otherwise, they will all descend on us here."

"Lady forbid," Riv'ella breathed, and Birlerion could only agree.

Birlerion called Ari as he walked back into the camp. Exhaustion swept through him, and he was glad he didn't have to do anything further; all he wanted to do was sleep. He collapsed beside Versillion, ignoring all his worried questions. When the little Arifel popped into view, Birlerion struggled to raise his head. *"Ari, tell Kayerille and Virenion that the Kirshans will bring us all to Rabat. Tell them to save their energy, and we'll meet them there."* He closed his eyes and fell asleep.

He was woken late the next morning by the arrival of Kayerille and Oscar. Kayerille knelt beside him. "Birlerion, are you alright? What happened to you?"

"Nothing. I'm fine," Birlerion croaked. He tried to swallow, but his throat felt like shards of glass were sticking out of it. Val'eria handed him a canteen.

"You don't look it," Oscar said, peering at him over

Kayerille's shoulder. "You look like someone beat you up and then came back and did it again."

"It's just bruising," Val'eria said. "It always looks worse when it first comes out. Being run over by a horse and attacked by a madwoman will do that for you."

Kayerille grimaced and glared at Versillion. "And you! What a pair you are. You are not safe to be left on your own."

"Everything is fine. The Kirshans offered to carry our wounded to Rabat. They are choosing their new Medera today. Things will get better now." Birlerion slowly sat up and rubbed his swollen neck. His throat was sore, his voice was a scratchy whisper, and his head ached. He gratefully took the draught Val'eria handed him.

"They already did. They are waiting to speak to you, but Val'eria wouldn't let you be disturbed until now," Kayerille said.

"Try and stay out of the sun as much as possible; it won't do your head any good," Val'eria said, watching him closely. His eyes were heavy, and under the bruising, he still looked pale.

"How is Maraine? Did you see her before you left?"

"She arrived not long after us. Viktor was relieved, I can tell you. She was fine; angry and a bit tired, but otherwise fine. They agreed to wait in Rabat as guests of Medera Reina until we brought you back."

"Birlerion needs to rest. He can't take much more," Val'eria said, sounding worried. "He should travel with Versillion. He can rest then."

Kayerille's eyebrows rose as Birlerion agreed without arguing.

"Let's get you cleaned up and to the Medera. Then you can lie back down again," Val'eria said.

Kin'arol's faint voice intruded. *"Rigs, you need to drink the water. It may be dirty, but it's all we've got."*

Birlerion stiffened. *"Kin'arol? Is that you? Where are you?"*

"Birlerion? We're being herded east. We are being chased. I go to Selir and then head south."

"I'm travelling to Rabat. When you get to Selir, stay there. Ask Rigs to find Roberion. He'll protect you. I'll warn him you are coming. I'll meet you there."

Birlerion refocussed on the tent. No one had noticed his distraction, so he rolled to his feet, trying to hide his weariness. "I'll just wash, and then we'll go," he murmured. Wrapping a scarf around his head, he left the tent, wincing as the glare of the sun hurt his eyes. There was enough water to clean his teeth and wash his face and hands. The rest would have to make do.

Glancing around, he realised he was alone. He called an Arifel, and immediately, Lin popped into view as if she had been waiting. *"Lin, go find Roberion. Tell him that Kino, my Darian, is approaching Selir from the west. He needs help. They are being chased by Kirshans who don't realise their Medera has changed her orders. The child with him is important; keep her safe. Tell him I'm on my way."*

The little Arifel chittered and disappeared.

Birlerion returned to the healer's tent. The sooner they were on the road, the better. Once he was in Rabat, he could use the waystone.

Yer'ota was waiting to escort him to the Kirshan camp when he arrived. Someone had clearly been tattling, because he gave Birlerion a searching inspection before they left.

"I'm fine," Birlerion murmured as they walked.

Yer'ota chuckled in response. "It's a good job you are hiding your face in those scarves, else no one would believe you."

"I just have a headache. Val'eria gave me something for it. I'll be fine."

"Then let's get you out of the sun. We'll load up your wounded and then we'll be off. The Medera has decreed we return to Rabat."

Birlerion was unsurprised to find Medera Rivella waiting for him in the last tent still standing. "Medera, congratulations."

Rivella's smile was faint. "I'm not sure congratulations is quite the right word, but thank you."

"You will bring honour back to Kirsha; of that, I am sure."

"I intend to. First, we need to get your men back to Rabat. Then we will see."

"Mederas Reina and Maraine are both in Rabat. And Commander Landis of the Terolian King's Guard has just arrived. You ought to know, some of his men were killed in the ambush on Maraine."

Rivella closed her eyes and took a deep breath. "Then maybe I ought to speak with him before we leave. I don't think I could face three antagonists at the same time."

Birlerion smiled. "You can face whatever you need to for Kirsha."

"Yes, but if I don't have to, then I won't. Yer'ota, would you be so good as to invite Commander Landis to come and speak to me?"

Yer'ota bowed himself out, and Rivella and Birlerion were left alone.

"I thank the Lady for sending you to us. Already there is a lighter atmosphere in camp. Until the burden is removed, you don't realise how much of an effect it has."

"I'm glad, and I'm also sorry that your hand had to strike your mother down."

Regret and anguish, quickly hidden, flashed across her face. "It was meant to be, and it had to be done. We are free now, and we will be better for it. Thank you, Birlerion." She held out her hand, and they shook. Her grip was firm, and he smiled at her. She smiled in return, her grave expression lightening. "We are in your debt."

"No, the Lady watches. I am but Her instrument, performing Her will. You owe me nothing."

"As the Lady wills. But still, Kirsha is here should you need us," Rivella said, and she turned as Yer'ota and Oscar arrived.

Birlerion bowed his way out. He found Versillion and joined him in the back of the wagon. Easing down with a groan, he laid his aching head on a cushion and closed his eyes.

He slept for most of the journey to Rabat, awakening a few times to take a gulp of water and accept another draught from Val'eria before dozing again. The soft rumble of Versillion's voice soothed Birlerion as his brother and Val'eria chatted. Birlerion listened for a moment; Versillion was extolling the beauties of Greens. He smiled at the enthusiasm in his brother's usually stoic voice and fell asleep again.

When he woke, he felt just as tired. Versillion and Val'eria were speaking in low tones and he deliberated about not moving as he realised they had moved on from generalities to a more intimate conversation, but he was unable to stay still any longer and as he stretched the voices stopped abruptly. When he sat up, they were a decent distance apart and he grimaced as he moved, his muscles protesting. He took a drink from his canteen and rinsed his face and then peered out the back of the wagon. The Kharma ridge was a shimmer on the horizon. They must nearly be at Rabat. He sat back down beside Versillion. "How are you feeling?"

Versillion grunted. "Be glad to get off this wagon. What about you? You look worse than me."

"I'm fine. I slept well. The bruising will fade; it's nothing.

How long does he have to be immobilised?" Birlerion asked Val'eria.

"At least another week or two, and then it will be another month with crutches."

Birlerion considered his brother. "Looks like you'll be staying with the Atolea for a while, then." He grinned. "Make sure you look after him, Val'eria. I look forward to seeing you in Greens."

"Birlerion!"

Versillion flushed red as Val'eria laughed. "I told you he wasn't asleep all the time."

"I'm happy for you both. Truly," Birlerion said with a sly grin as he observed his brother's agonised face.

"Don't say anything, please. We'll announce it in our own time," Versillion pleaded.

"Of course I won't. Bet you're glad you came to Terolia now, aren't you, brother?"

Versillion groaned. "He's going to take the credit for this. We'll never hear the end of it," he said and the wagon came to a stop.

20

Birlerion smiled in welcome as Mir'elle sneaked into the tent to sit next to him. "Will you tell me who everyone is? I've never met the Solari or the Kirshan."

"Of course," Birlerion murmured, casting a glance around the tent. Rivella was seated next to Reina, and they were deep in conversation with Maraine. They glanced in his direction often, and he wondered what they were saying about him.

"Umm, if you're not supposed to be here, sitting next to me might not be a good choice," he said.

Mir'elle laughed and cast a sparkling glance up at him that made him catch his breath. "My mother would expect me to make the most of this opportunity, and you, brother, are the best escort."

Birlerion grinned. "Why, thank you, sister dear. In that case, let me tell you that your mother and Mederas Reina and Rivella are the most important people in the room." Mir'elle's peal of laughter caught everyone's attention.

"Oops," she said, covering her mouth.

"The next most important are your father and Sodera Tomas."

Mir'elle rolled her eyes.

"After them, a new political player, I would suggest, is Commander Landis. You should make his acquaintance."

Mir'elle squinted at the commander seated next to Kayerille. "Why?"

"Because he has the voice of King Benedict."

"And you don't?"

"Me? Goodness, no."

"But you have the Lady's Voice."

Birlerion laughed. "No, not me."

Mir'elle gave him a look of disbelief. "Of course you do. It's obvious. She values you."

Birlerion tilted his head. "What makes you say that?"

Mir'elle patted his arm. "Birlerion, you wouldn't be here if she didn't, and Kirsha listened to you."

"I suppose, but that doesn't mean I have her Voice."

"Yes, you do. You are here. You are always where you need to be, and you always make a difference."

Birlerion was silenced.

"You have a fan," Kin'arol murmured, and Birlerion tried hard not to laugh.

"Where are you?"

"Nearly at Selir."

"How is Rigs doing?"

"She is holding on, but she is tired."

"Are you sure you can make it to Selir?"

"We are still being chased, but we are nearly there."

Mir'elle stilled as Birlerion stiffened beside her. She recognised the expression on his face and moved to shield him from the rest of the tent. She watched him intently.

"Roberion is looking out for you."

"We go. They found our trail."

Birlerion called Ari.

He rose, and Mir'elle followed him out of the tent. Kayerille saw them leaving and followed.

Mir'elle gasped as Ari appeared and settled in Birlerion's hand. She extended a tentative finger to stroke his chest. He coyly ducked his head so that her fingers found his ears, and she laughed as he rubbed against her hand.

"This is Ari. He's an Arifel."

"He is so cute," she murmured. Ari butted her hand to keep it stroking.

"He is a time-waster. *Ari, tell Roberion that Kino and the child are still being chased. He needs to be ready to protect them.*"

Ari chittered and disappeared.

"Mir'elle, thank you for your company, but I need to leave." He glanced behind her. "Kayerille, we need to take the waystone to Selir."

"Birlerion, you can't."

"Of course I can. I'm fine. It's been months. Kino is being chased. He needs help."

"Now?"

"Yes, now. I'm not waiting any longer."

"But you have to address the conclave tomorrow."

"We'll be back by then."

"No, I'll go. I'll bring him back."

Birlerion gritted his teeth. "I won't break. I am fine, and I am going."

"*Birlerion, no. Roberion will bring us to you. Don't take any risks for me.*"

"*It is no risk, and, if necessary, I would risk everything for you.*"

Mir'elle glanced at Birlerion's face. "He's telling you no, isn't he? Please don't go, Birlerion."

"*How far from Selir are you?*"

"*We approach now.*"

"*You come straight here.*"

"I come."

Birlerion released his breath. "I'll wait for an hour. If he isn't here by then, I'll go."

Kayerille exhaled as well. "Fine. Let's join Oscar. He needs some support. I think he is overwhelmed by all these Mederas in one place."

"You go. I'll be there in a minute."

When Kayerille hesitated, Birlerion grinned. "You don't trust me?"

She twisted her lips. "You always make your own decisions, Birlerion. It never seems like it, but you do. That's what I love about you. You know your own mind, but you know what I think. I don't want to lose you."

"You won't. I promise."

Mir'elle grasped Kayerille's hand. "You can trust my brother. He would not lie."

Kayerille stared at him and then nodded in resigned acceptance before turning away and walking with Mir'elle towards Medera Reina's tent.

Birlerion sighed and stared out across the empty sands, listening for Kin'arol. The night was still, the fragrant air cooling fast. Kin'arol's voice soothed the empty space in his chest. He still felt displaced; no matter what he did, it didn't feel right. If he were being honest, he missed his adopted father, Warren, his anchor, the one who helped everything make sense. And he missed Leyandrii. She had always been there, a presence at his shoulder. This new distance was uncomfortable, as if he had lost something that completed him.

Common sense said it was because he was still recovering from a major injury. He shouldn't even be alive; that was mind-blowing in itself. Of course he felt unsettled. He had a second chance. He shouldn't waste it. He also shouldn't take silly risks. And he should be behind Jerrol's shoulder, protecting him. Getting himself killed wouldn't help the Lady's Captain.

"Good choice," Kin'arol murmured, and Birlerion smiled to himself. His Darian had been monitoring his thoughts. They didn't need to bond; they already knew each other. And he wasn't alone anymore; Kin'arol was with him.

He turned away from the desert and walked towards the tent.

Kayerille relaxed as Birlerion ducked in the flap, and Oscar raised an eyebrow at her. She squeezed his hand and smiled. "What?" Oscar breathed.

"Nothing," Kayerille replied.

Oscar followed her gaze and spotted Birlerion sitting down beside Mir'elle. He dipped his head next to hers. "What happened?"

"Nothing yet. Just keep an eye on Birlerion for me. His Darian is in trouble. Tell me if he leaves."

The air shimmered, and Ari appeared before her, clutching a message. "Well done, Ari," she said as she took the message, and then he popped out of sight.

"What is it?" Oscar asked.

"Message for you from Rin'urda."

"Nice to know the process works," Oscar murmured, taking the note. He unrolled it and peered at the tiny writing.

"A new sentinal tree has appeared in Tesene." He wrinkled his nose. "Why would a sentinal appear now?"

"I have no idea, but we need to tell the Captain. He'll need to wake them up."

"It'll take him weeks to reach Tesene."

"I doubt there's a rush. They'll be waiting when the Captain gets there."

21

Concentration eluded him. Birlerion tried, but he couldn't focus on the conversation swirling around him. His whole purpose for being here was to get Kin'arol. Sitting here socialising whilst his Darian was in difficulty grated on his protective sensibilities.

Maraine leaned over. "What is the matter, Birlerion? You seem distracted."

"Nothing. It's just—"

"Birlerion!"

The moment Kin'arol's voice sliced through him, Birlerion was on his feet. His heart raced at the fear in his Darian's voice.

"There are more. They force us south. Birlerion, I can't reach Selir. We need water."

"I'm coming. Head for Tesene. Hang on, Kin'arol. I will bring water."

"Hurry."

"What is wrong, Birlerion?" Maraine asked.

"It's my Darian. He was headed for Selir, but he is being chased by Kirshans. They are forcing them south. They can't reach Selir, and they are running out of water. I need to get to Tesene."

"Them?" Rivella asked.

"A child called Rigs is with him. He said she can speak with him. I think she helped him escape, but I'm not sure."

Rivella and Reina exchanged glances. "A child who can bespeak Darians?"

"Do you think?" Rivella asked.

Reina shrugged. "It's well past time. It's possible."

"Then we need to find her. Birlerion, where did you say they were?"

"South of Selir. They are being forced south. Tesene is the only village I know out that way."

"Tesene?" Oscar said. "I just got word that a new sentinal tree has appeared there."

Birlerion swung around, the need to act singing in his veins. "I have to get to Tesene."

Kayerille barred his way. "Not on your own. They are being chased, you said, and it sounds like there are many of them."

"We will go with you." Rivella said. "They are my family. They may be misguided, but they are family. They will listen to me. Yer'ota, prepare the men. We ride as soon as we are ready."

A soft voice rippled in Birlerion's mind. *"I will take you. Kin'arol needs our help."* It was the bay Darian Rigs had asked to help him.

He spun, searching the tent, and then met Rivella's eyes. She nodded, her eyes distant as she spoke with her Darian. "Take him if he is willing. It is a good sign that Ger'inne is prepared to help. We were concerned he may refuse to speak to us."

Oscar observed them with a crease between his brows and blew out his breath as he shrugged, resigned to being excluded from the silent conversations going on around him. "Mederas, I think this is an opportunity to show the unity of the Terolian guards. I will take a mixed unit with me if you agree," Oscar suggested.

Maraine stared at him. "Excellent idea, Commander. Let us start as we mean to go on."

"We have to move fast. We may end up in a skirmish in the middle of the desert. Travel rations and extra water only. Nothing else." Birlerion strode out of the tent.

Oscar grimaced. "Keeping up with him will be the problem."

Viktor stood. "I'll speak to him. His urgency is understandable, but arriving with no one fit to fight would be a waste of time. You prepare your men. I'll prepare my son." He nodded and followed Birlerion.

Within the hour, they were ready.

Birlerion hugged Versillion in farewell. "I'll send word as soon as we get Kino."

"You be careful. No stupid heroics. Let Oscar's men prove themselves."

"I've already had the lecture from Viktor. Don't worry. I will take care. It's only a day to Tesene. Hopefully, he'll be there, waiting for us."

"Lady bless you, Birlerion."

"And you, brother."

Birlerion met the bay Darian at the head of the column. He rechecked everything, including the canteens of water tied to his saddle.

"My name is Ger'inne."

"Ger'inne, thank you for letting me ride you."

"I help."

"Yes, you do." Birlerion rubbed the muscular neck, so powerful and strong. He leaned his head against Ger'inne's

and breathed in the musky scent of the Darian, which he had missed for so long. Tense muscles relaxed.

"You will be with him soon," Ger'inne said.

"Yes, Lady willing."

Oscar stopped beside him and gripped his arm. "Ready?"

"Always," Birlerion replied. He straightened, and Oscar nodded.

"Lead the way, then."

Birlerion led the column of Terolian guards and Kirshan patrol, led by Rivella and Yer'ota, out into the night-shrouded desert. He set a steady pace, one the Terolians could maintain for hours.

He listened for Kin'arol as they travelled, letting Ger'inne pick his path. The waning moon glistened overhead, lighting up the rolling desert. Ger'inne kept up the pace, and as Birlerion glanced over his shoulder to check his column, the Darian chuckled in his head.

"They follow. They won't let you out of their sight."

"I suppose not. How far do you think we'll get before we have to stop?"

"After four hours, it's best to rest for an hour. Even though it's cool now, we'll travel better for having had a drink and a rest. We should reach Tesene by sunup."

Birlerion called Kin'arol. *"We should be at Tesene by sunup."*

"Meet us north of the Tesene hills. We will not make the town."

"I'm coming, Kin'arol. Where are the Kirshans?"

"They follow. I hear them. They draw closer. I tire."

"Don't stop, Kin'arol. I'm sure they are just as tired as you are."

"I come."

Birlerion reluctantly called a halt. He filled a leather bag with water and offered it to Ger'inne. Once the Darian had had his fill, Birlerion stowed it all away. Chewing on a strip of dried meat, he strolled over to Kayerille and Oscar. "Kino says they are closing in on him. By dawn, he will be north of the Tesene hills. I think we should arrange a welcoming committee."

Yer'ota joined them. His teeth gleamed in the moonlight as he grinned. "The Medera is eager to speak to them."

"I think you need to concentrate on Kino. As soon as you see him, your job is to look after him. Leave the Kirshans to the rest of us." Oscar glanced at Yer'ota and the swarthy Solari Sodera, Tomas, who had accompanied them. "You know this land better than I. What do you suggest?"

"How far does he think they are behind him?" Sodera Tomas asked.

"He can hear them, so they are close."

Tomas nodded, his eyes distant. "I have a Darian. We will know as soon as Kino comes within range. If the commander agrees, I will take half of the men and sweep around behind them. Medera, you meet them head on, and if they don't stop to listen, we will have them surrounded and we will grind them between us."

Rivella nodded. "I agree. They have but one chance to listen. If they are not prepared to heed my word, then they forfeit their right to be heard."

"Clemency in action," Oscar murmured under his breath, though not quite low enough for Rivella flashed him a vicious grin. "How many of your family are missing, Medera? What are we facing?"

"My uncle and his two sons and their men. My mother allowed him his own patrol; a mistake, it seems. They can't number more than ten, though ten can still cause damage." She looked around the Terolians with them. "Our sons have been led astray; they believe what they do is right as they fulfil their Medera's wishes. I must give them the chance to understand that the order has changed. But if they will not listen and the Darian and the child are at risk, then we must act.

"If they won't throw down their weapons and surrender, then do whatever you need to do to restrain them. Kirsha will not demand retribution for any action taken here."

The men nodded and returned to their mounts, and in very little time, they were on their way again.

The sky was beginning to lighten when the village of Tesene appeared on the horizon, the hills rising behind it.

"Kino, I see Tesene and the hills."

"I can't."

"Ger'inne, tell Tomas that Kino still can't see the hills. He must be further out than we thought. He is tiring."

"Tomas says to get to the other side of the hills."

Ger'inne picked up his pace. They skirted the village, the tall sentinal tree standing prominently where previously there had been none, and they scrambled over the hills. More desert rolled out in front of them all the way to the sea.

"They didn't reach Selir, so they must be further west."

"I see the hills." Kin'arol's voice was faint.

"I hear him. He is that way." Ger'inne turned to the west.

Tomas waved his hand above his head and headed east.

Ger'inne led the rest in a flat-out gallop towards Kino's voice, which scared Birlerion more than anything else. He bent low and hung on.

Kin'arol was barely walking by the time they found him, staggering in a southerly direction, a small bundle on his back. He faltered to a stop as Birlerion slid out of his saddle, pouring water into the bag as he ran. He slung it around Kin'arol's neck.

"Kin'arol."

"Birlerion, I am here." Kin'arol's rich voice filled Birlerion's mind as he hugged the exhausted Darian. A sense of belonging infused him and locked into place. Kin'arol's

weary thoughts embraced him, warmed him, and their bond united them, one to the other, for always and forever. A gentle presence permeated his mind, filling the lonely gaps and absorbing all his attention as it settled, joining his sentinal's hum in joyous completion. He would never be alone again.

Birlerion hid his face in Kin'arol's scratchy mane as tears threatened to overwhelm him. He inhaled the comforting aroma of his Darian as he accepted all that Kin'arol offered. Emotions overflowing, he returned the greeting and Kin'arol, in turn, embraced all that he was. *"I am so pleased to finally meet you. I've missed you."*

"I am glad, too." Kin'arol replied.

Birlerion took a deep breath and looked up. "You must be Rig'asol." He wiped his face and peered up at the child perched on Kin'arol's back. "Are you alright?"

Rig'asol wrinkled her nose. "He made me drink dirty water."

Birlerion laughed. "Dirty water is better than no water. Come, we have clean water." He reached up and she slid into his arms. She was tiny and weighed nothing, and Birlerion hugged her before letting her go. He knelt down beside her and offered her the canteen. She sighed with relief and drank long and deep.

"Thank you, Rig'asol, for looking after him. I owe you for my Darian's life."

"No, you don't. He's yours and no one else's. It wasn't right what they did."

"No, it wasn't, but being on your own in the desert can be dangerous. Your family must be worried about you."

Rig'asol shrugged, unconcerned. "He looked after me; he made me wash in the river."

Kin'arol's relief percolated through him as he drank his

fill, and Birlerion refilled the water sack and offered it to Ger'inne.

"I waited, but you never came, and then others did."

"I am sorry I didn't come in time. I was delayed."

"You were ill. You are better now."

Birlerion rubbed Kin'arol's neck. *"What did they do to your coat? It feels horrible."*

Rig'asol's much younger voice interrupted them. *"They dyed it to disguise him. It will grow out. I have been brushing him."*

Birlerion looked over his dirty grey stallion, and Kin'arol folded into the sand, his head too heavy to hold up any longer. Birlerion uncinched Ger'inne's saddle, and the Darian knelt next to Kin'arol, propping him up. Kin'arol lay his head across Ger'inne's neck and groaned.

Rigs crouched beside him and stroked his neck.

"You must be exhausted, too, Rigs."

"Not as much as him. He had to carry both of us, and it's been very hot," she said, hugging the water skin. Birlerion offered her some dried fruit, and she nibbled it daintily.

The Terolians set up a perimeter, though many peered at the cause of all the trouble. The horse didn't look like a Darian.

Birlerion arranged a crude awning, enough to keep the sun off, and began making a moist mash. It reminded him of another Darian he had once been sent to rescue in the desert. Der'inder, the sire of Kaf'enir's foal. He concentrated on feeding it to Kin'arol, along with more water.

"Eat this now and later you can have some baliweed. I brought some especially."

Ger'inne jerked his head up. *"Me, too?"*

"A true rider," Kin'arol murmured, swallowing the mash.

Birlerion grinned and kept stuffing the mash in his Darian's mouth.

At last, Kin'arol heaved a satisfied sigh.

"Kin'arol?"

"I'm sleeping, as should you."

Rigs chuckled and curled up next to him.

Birlerion settled beside them and closed his eyes. For once, someone else could do the fighting.

22

T he sound of fighting drawing closer woke Birlerion. He lay for a moment listening, and then groaned as tired muscles protested as he rose and unsheathed his bow. Wrapping his scarves around his face, he scrambled out of the awning. Glancing back, he saw Rigs watching him, wide-eyed. "Stay with Kino. You are safe here."

"Then why are you leaving?"

Birlerion grimaced at the question. "Just making sure."

The sun had risen and now burned down from a perfectly clear blue sky. The sands were baking, and the heat was intense. He observed the fighting as he strung his bow. If anyone came within range, he would shoot them.

He stood over his Darian and watched the darting runs of the Solari, so distinctive and very effective. Oscar's men needed to train more together with the Families, but that was expected being so new to the territory. Each Family had their own strengths, and the fact that they were working together spoke volumes about Oscar's command of the situation.

And yet the fight was still coming in Birlerion's direction.

He squinted. The Kirshans were engaging and falling back, dragging the fight towards Tesene. Why did they want

Kin'arol so badly? Enough to ignore the words of their Medera and sacrifice their lives?

Birlerion nocked an arrow, sighted, and released. It was easy, really. The ground was open, nothing to get in the way. He nocked another arrow and waited for the next victim to come into range.

As the second body fell, the Kirshans were not the only ones to flick a glance over their shoulders in concern.

Birlerion frowned as he watched. There were more than ten of them. Had they collected some paid help along the way? Again, why were they so determined?

"Kin'arol?"

"Yes?" His Darian's voice was sleepy.

"Sorry to wake you, but what did you do in Fuertes to make them so determined?"

"I didn't do anything. It was Rigs."

"What did Rigs do?"

"She made every Darian help us escape. They all obeyed her."

"She can speak with all Darians?"

"Yes, I can." Rig'asol's voice was light but determined. *"But I only* asked *them to help us, nothing else."*

"I'm glad you did, Rigs, and I thank you." Birlerion adjusted his thinking. They were after Rigs, not Kin'arol. Birlerion had never heard of anyone being able to talk to all Darians. They must have switched targets, though it made little difference with them together.

"Ger'inne, can you tell Tomas that they are after the child?"

"Done," Ger'inne replied.

"Kin'arol, do you think you can stand? We need to get to the other side of the hills."

"If I have to."

Birlerion winced in sympathy at the exhaustion in Kin'arol's voice. *"Only to the other side. The hills will provide some protection. Then you can go back to sleep."*

"Alright." Kin'arol struggled to his feet, and the awning collapsed around him. *"Sorry."*

Birlerion slung the saddle on Ger'inne, cinched it tight, and tossed Rigs on his back. He bundled the awning up and tied it to the back of the saddle. *"Ger'inne, get us over the hills. Kin'arol, follow. I'll be right behind you."*

Covering their retreat, Birlerion followed the horses as they made their way back through the hills. He lay on the crest of the highest hill and watched the fight draw to a close. When the last men standing were surrounded and threw down their arms, he breathed a sigh of relief and scrambled down the hill to erect the awning over Kin'arol, who had collapsed in the sand. Rigs was trying to get him to drink more water.

"Tell Tomas where we are."

"He comes," Ger'inne replied.

Birlerion lifted Kin'arol's head, and the Darian managed to drink some more water. Ger'inne wedged himself behind Kin'arol, propping him up. Birlerion rubbed his neck. *"Sleep, my friend. You are safe now."*

Kin'arol shuddered and nudged Birlerion. *"I am so tired."*

"I know. Ger'inne and I will keep watch. Sleep."

Once Tomas had arrived and a new perimeter had been set, Birlerion settled down, and with Rigs in his arms, they fell asleep.

Kayerille looked down at them, a jumble of man and horses, and grinned. Birlerion lay wedged between two Darians, and in his arms a tiny child slept. "Alright for some, eh?" she said to Oscar, who paused beside her.

He chuckled. "Like innocent babes."

"Very trusting. Most unusual for Birlerion."

"I don't want to move." Kin'arol's voice was a whisper in his mind.

"*Don't, then. No rush. Others watch,*" Birlerion replied, ignoring those standing over them.

"*Good,*" Kin'arol mumbled, and silence fell.

Dusk had fallen when the aroma of roasting meat wafted on the evening air, and Birlerion opened his eyes and inhaled. His crude awning had been surrounded by wagons and tents and he hadn't heard a thing.

Rigs was no longer sleeping in his arms, and Ger'inne was standing over them. Kin'arol had shifted around him, and Birlerion now lay curled against his neck.

"*Are you awake?*" Birlerion asked Kin'arol.

"*Yes, I've been watching them arrive. You were very tired.*"

"*I would have thought you were the tired one, not me.*"

"*I think you worry, and now there is no reason to worry. You sleep.*"

Birlerion sat up, and Kin'arol shuddered to his feet.

"*I am stiff,*" he complained.

"*I'll give you a good rubdown. That will help.*"

"*Thank you. Could I have another drink?*"

"*Of course.*" Birlerion hunted around and found a full bucket to the side. "*Have they been topping you up?*"

"*Yes. They thought it was funny that you didn't wake.*"

Birlerion sighed. "*They would.*"

He stared around him. Rolling sand dunes filled the horizon; the desert an endless expanse of sand. Hues of gold and umber shimmered into the yellow of the sky. Colourful wagons and tents crowded around them, all the way up to the outskirts of the village of Tesene. A small dusty village of golden stone houses huddled around the life-giving oasis in the centre, now graced by the tall sentinal tree. "*Did everyone move here from Rabat?*"

"*I don't know who was in Rabat.*"

Birlerion laughed. *"Of course you don't. Never mind. I'm starving. Let me eat, and then I'll rub you down."*

"We'll join the others now that you're awake," Kin'arol said, and he followed Birlerion through the camp, with Ger'inne behind him. Kin'arol nodded his head with fatigue as he walked.

Children laughed as they passed, pointing at the horses following the man.

A young Terolian lad with flashing brown eyes led them to the picket and offered a hay net. With a double *"Ahh … baliweed,"* sighing through his head, Birlerion went in search of food. He grinned at Kin'arol's sigh of bliss as the lad began to groom his coat, ridding him of the dust and grime of their journey. The Darian's hum of satisfaction filled Birlerion's mind, and he relaxed.

He followed his nose and found the roast—and the rest of the rescue party. He dropped into a seat beside Oscar. "How did it go?"

"As planned. They were all suitably chastised by their Medera. Quite boring, really, having travelled all night."

"Boring is best," Birlerion replied, accepting a plate of flatbread covered in strips of meat and stringent mint sauce. "A few more than expected, though."

"Yes, that's what caused the problem. Those not of the Family didn't understand what was being offered, and they forced the hands of those who did."

"What made everyone come here? I thought they were settled in Rabat."

"They didn't want to make you and Kino travel all the way to Rabat only to have to come back again to reach Roberion's ship. Roberion is going to take you home as originally planned."

Birlerion lurched up. "Roberion? Where is he?"

"He's talking with Versillion, so eat your dinner. You can see him after."

"Where's Rigs?"

"Mir'elle is looking after her. They seem to be getting on quite well," Maraine said from above him. She waved him back as he started to rise. "Eat, Birlerion. I know you've slept all day. Is that what it takes to get a man to sleep? Threaten his Darian? I'll have to remember that."

Birlerion grinned. "I didn't realise I was so tired."

"We told you often enough. But you slept, and you look much better for it."

"That is because he has his Darian," Viktor said as he eased himself down beside Maraine.

"I'm sorry to drag you all out this way," Birlerion said.

"Oscar needed to visit; it's another town he can cross off his list," Maraine said comfortably.

Kayerille laughed as she handed Maraine a mug. "Kafinee?" she asked, holding out another mug.

"Thank you." Birlerion took it, inhaled, and sipped.

Settling on the rug beside Oscar, Kayerille peered at Birlerion. "Do you know who is in the sentinal?"

Birlerion stilled. "I haven't checked. I was so focused on Kino I never even thought." He opened his mind and felt the name chime through him. "Edrilion," he murmured.

"I wondered," Kayerille said, her voice equally soft. Only Birlerion could tell who was in the Sentinal without touching it.

"He sleeps still. The Captain will have to wake him."

"Will he be alright, do you think? I mean, why has he only now appeared?"

"Maybe banishing the Ascendants for good broke whatever was keeping him hidden?" Birlerion stared at the starry sky. Edrilion had been enspelled by the Ascendants at one time. Only Marguerite had been able to release him. Who knew what had happened to him. He looked around at the others and shrugged. "I suppose we'll find out when he wakes."

Mir'elle and Rigs interrupted them, and the subject changed to Darians, of course.

After dinner, Birlerion and Rigs strolled along the picket line.

Rigs peered at the horses. "There you are." She reached up and petted the bay stallion.

Birlerion stroked his neck. *"I am sorry for your loss, but I thank you for your help."*

"I helped."

"You did. You did well."

"Thank you for saving Birlerion." Kin'arol's voice was soft.

Ger'inne whickered and tossed his head as Yer'ota appeared out of the dark to join them. "She really is an Eleve," he said.

"An Eleve?"

"Eleves can speak to all Darians. They are rare and much sought after."

"She is also a little girl who ought to rest. Rigs, let's settle Kino, and then you can sleep."

Rigs snorted as she peered up at Kin'arol. "Kino suits him," she said as she ducked under his legs and dragged a bucket of water over to him. Kin'arol dipped his head into the bucket and drank deeply.

"I'm here. You are not alone. Look after Rigs. She is tired, though she won't admit it." Kin'arol's voice caressed Birlerion, and the tension left his body.

"Are you from Fuertes, Rig'asol?" Birlerion asked, keeping his voice even as he led her over to the fire outside the healer's tent. It was much quieter than the main camp, and Kayerille and Oscar sat on the cushions, heads together, speaking in low voices.

Ignoring them he picked a cushion opposite and made himself comfortable.

Rigs flicked a sharp glance at him. "Call me Rigs."

"Rigs, where is your family?"

She flushed, and her black eyes glittered with tears. Kin'arol's nicker of comfort was clear on the night air. "They are not my family. They took Kino."

"Why don't you tell me what happened?" Birlerion asked.

"I knew when they tied him up that it was all wrong. He was upset. I could feel it."

Yer'ota joined them by the fire, offering more platters of food.

Rig'asol inspected the tray, and after choosing some baked vegetables and bread, she sat close to Birlerion. She ate as daintily as she appeared.

"Where were you camped?"

"In Livia. We were just moving on to Melila."

"Who brought Kino to your camp?"

"My brothers. They called him a bad horse. He bit Viv; he deserved it." Rigs tore off a piece of bread with her teeth, and Birlerion smiled.

"What did they intend to do with him?"

"My pa wanted one of them to bond with him," Rigs said with a snort. "Even he could see there was no chance of that. Kino wouldn't let any of them touch him."

"And then?" Birlerion prompted.

"Pa said to cut our losses and sell him."

"But why go all the way up to Fuertes? They could have sold him to anyone."

Rigs shrugged. "I don't know."

"They thought to hide me amongst the others. The Atolea wouldn't find me there. Not that it worked," Kin'arol said.

"Do you know why they stole you in the first place?"

"Pa said it was wrong to send him out of the desert," Rigs said.

"Silva wanted revenge on Maraine," Kin'arol added, his voice sad.

"Is your family affiliated with Kirsha, Rigs?"

Rigs hunched over on her cushion.

"Rigs." Birlerion's voice was soft. "There is no shame in being Kirshan."

"Yes, there is. They do bad stuff."

"Not all of them, and some of those who did do bad things only did them because they thought they were doing the right thing. Hey, don't cry." Birlerion dragged her onto his lap and hugged her tight. "You didn't do a bad thing. You helped Kino at great risk to yourself. Rigs, you are very special." He rocked her gently. *"You are very special, and don't ever let anyone tell you differently. You were very brave to take Kin'arol out into the desert."*

Yer'ota knelt beside them. "Rig'asol, you bring honour to the Kirsha family. I thank you for saving Kino. Our Family has been misled, but now we have a new mother, whom you can be proud to call Medera. You'll see. Kirsha's honour will be restored, and it is because we have daughters like you that Kirsha will flourish."

Rigs sighed against Birlerion's chest and gripped his robe more tightly. *"I want to stay with you and Kin'arol."*

"And you would be welcome, but I think the Lady has bigger plans for you. You would not be able to talk to all Darians without reason. Would you not prefer to work with a lot of Darians all the time?"

Rigs lifted her head. *"A lot?"*

Birlerion smiled. *"You could work with the herds in Fuertes if you wanted to."*

"We would visit you," Kin'arol offered.

Ger'inne's voice intruded, *"So would I."*

"What are they saying?" Oscar whispered.

Yer'ota grinned. "I think they are negotiating."

"*I would be honoured to be your friend,*" Birlerion offered.

"*My brother,*" Rigs replied.

"*If you insist.*" Birlerion laughed and glanced around the fire. "My family grows. Sorry. Rigs and I were just discussing her future career."

"And?" Yer'ota asked.

"I think you may need to sponsor her into the Solari heartlands."

"I doubt there will be any difficulty with that."

Rigs stared at him. "Are you going to be the new Sodera?"

Yer'ota laughed. "No, not me. Others are wiser than me."

"It *should* be you. You would be good for Kirsha."

"Out of the mouth of babes," a light voice said from behind them.

They all looked up, startled, and Medera Rivella approached out of the shadows. The torches caressed her smooth skin and glossy black hair twirled upon her head. The Kirshan tattoo gleamed on her cheek, along with the vivid orange flame.

Yer'ota sprang to his feet. "Medera!"

"I believe I have arrived just at the right time. There is much to be discussed, and Yer'ota, I need you." Rivella caught Yer'ota's eyes.

Yer'ota's shoulders stiffened, but he nodded. "Let me introduce you to Rig'asol. She has brought Birlerion's Darian home."

Birlerion rose with Rigs still in his arms. "Medera, Lady's greetings."

Rivella inspected him for a moment, her black eyes intent. "I am glad you are reunited with your Darian, and I thank you for caring for a daughter of the Family." Her gaze moved to Rigs, and her face relaxed into a beautiful smile.

"Dearest Rigs, I think you are way past your bedtime. Would you like to come and stay with me?"

Rigs considered her. "If I can see Birlerion and Kino tomorrow."

"Of course." Rivella's smile encompassed them all as Birlerion put her down. "You keep high company, I see. Until tomorrow." She swung Rigs into her arms, ignoring Yer'ota's offers to take her, and they walked back to the Kirshan camp.

"Did that actually just happen?" Kayerille asked as the dark night absorbed the Kirshans.

"I think so," Birlerion replied with a grin.

"What? What happened? Were you talking silently again? What did I miss?" Oscar scowled. "You know, that can get really annoying."

Kayerille's laugh pealed out, and she hugged him. "Oscar, dear, you can be so obtuse sometimes."

As Oscar stared at her, a slow smile crept over his face. He slid his arms around her waist and tugged her close. "What?" he said in an injured tone, and he kissed her.

"The Medera just claimed her Sodera," Kayerille said and then kissed him back.

Birlerion faded into the shadows and made his way towards the healerie. He ducked under the flap.

Roberion looked up from his seat beside Versillion, his large frame filling the space. "Birlerion. Lad, I hear you have been causing trouble as usual."

"Me? I don't cause trouble."

Roberion gripped his arm. "I am glad to see you well."

"Thank you. I feel much better. Roberion, thank you for being prepared to help Kino. I appreciate it."

"Anytime. I am ready to take you back to Vespers on the *Miracle* whenever you want."

"Thank you. I think we need to wait for Jerrol to wake

Edrilion first. I'm sure there is a reason we are all here. Versillion, though, will need to stay here in the capable hands of Val'eria." Birlerion grinned. "Which I am sure won't be too much of a hardship."

Roberion's deep laugh rumbled through the tent as Versillion flushed.

"Let's find you a bed, Roberion, and leave him to cool down. We have a busy day tomorrow."

"*You* have a busy day tomorrow," Versillion said. "You're the one causing all the ructions."

"Me? Don't be silly. Roberion, let's go before he blames me for being stuck in here when that was all his fault."

Versillion's glare followed them out of the tent.

Birlerion cast a glance towards the fire but it was deserted.

23

The next morning after the Conclave, Birlerion stood by his Darian, frowning. "It looks terrible and feels even worse," he said, smoothing Kin'arol's coat.

"I know. I wish it would grow faster. It feels just as horrible," Kin'arol replied, tossing his head. His mane had about two inches of regrowth, a glossy black against the grubby grey. His coat looked matte and mottled and just wrong.

Rigs came scampering up. "We need to wash him every week. It will help."

Birlerion watched her run her hands over the Darian's legs and grinned at Kin'arol. *"The expert has spoken."*

"Then we should listen," Kin'arol replied, ducking his head so that Rigs could hug him.

"The Medera said she would speak to Medera Reina for me," Rigs said, jigging about. She couldn't keep still. "Isn't it exciting? Yer'ota is going to become the new Sodera. I told you."

"That is very exciting," Birlerion said, trying to keep his face straight. "But don't go bothering them. They are very busy right now."

"Not too busy for an Eleve," Yer'ota said from behind

them. "Reina is ecstatic. There hasn't been an Eleve for many years. The elder is failing. If she doesn't pass on her knowledge soon, it could be lost, and we would lose the ability to breed Darians." He grinned at Rigs, still hopping about like a sandfly. "Rigs is about to make history *and* secure our relations with the Solari."

"Well done, Rigs, and I hear more congratulations are in order. It seems to be in the air." Birlerion grasped Yer'ota's hand. "I wish you much happiness, my friend."

Yer'ota ran his other hand through his hair. "Rivella is insistent. I but obey my Medera's command."

Birlerion burst out laughing. "Liar," he said as he pulled Yer'ota into a hug.

Rigs stared up at them. "I'll join with you, Birlerion, when I'm old enough. Then it will be your turn."

Birlerion dropped into the sand beside Rigs. "It would be my honour to join with one such as you, but there is plenty of time for decisions like that. You have a new life to explore, and who knows what is on your horizon?" He punched her gently on the shoulder. "Anyway, you named me brother. You can't join with your brother."

"True, and you'll always be my brother; at least that will never change." Rigs hugged him and happily returned to Kin'arol. She ducked under his belly and greeted Ger'inne. "You know, Sodera, you ought to have a Darian, and this fellow here is lonely. I think the two of you will do well together." She untethered the bay and tugged him around to Yer'ota. "Don't you think so?" She smiled up at him, her black eyes lit by an inner glow.

Yer'ota held a trembling hand out to the Darian, and the bay ducked his head against it. Yer'ota exhaled in surprise as his eyes unfocused and his Darian greeted him. His arms crept around the Darian's neck, and he hid his face in Ger'inne's mane. Birlerion blinked away rising tears as he watched, and he rubbed Kin'arol's nose. *"We should have seen that one coming."*

"Ger'inne will look after him."

"I'm sure they will look after each other."

Yer'ota raised his head and met Birlerion's sympathetic eyes. "Birlerion, I am so sorry we delayed this for you for so long."

"I have him now. That is all that matters. I think Kirsha is in good hands, and with the support of the Solari and the Atolea, I am sure all will be well." He patted Kin'arol. "We can go home soon."

~

The next morning, the chime of a new waystone had the Sentinals rising and looking east. Niallerion and Jerrol stepped out into the desert.

A murmur rippled around the Terolians as Birlerion went to greet them. "Jerrol, I hear congratulations are in order. A son! Well done. I hope Taelia and the babe are well?"

Jerrol laughed and returned his embrace. "They are both fine, thank you. You look much better. Your Darian has made all the difference."

"He has, indeed," Birlerion replied as he clasped Niallerion's arm. "Medera Rivella and Maraine are still here, though the Solari left earlier this morning."

Jerrol cast him a glance. "You've been busy. I thought you were supposed to be recuperating?"

"I am. They still won't let me use the waystones. It is very frustrating. Val'eria is making me return home with Roberion on his ship. She doesn't trust me." Birlerion grimaced.

"Why am I not surprised?" Jerrol replied. "How is Versillion?"

"Healing, but then he has Val'eria keeping a close eye on him."

"He does, does he?" Jerrol smiled as the thin-faced captain stepped forward. "Oscar! Terolia suits you, I see."

"It does, indeed. We are making excellent progress. I have much to discuss with you."

Jerrol grimaced. "I'm sure you do, and I owe you an apology. I did not mean to send you out here so ill-prepared."

Oscar laughed. "Fortunately, Birlerion and Kayerille have looked after us. Without them, I would be complaining very loudly."

"I am saved, then. Thank the Lady. She was watching over us."

"She did say you were distracted by the impending birth of your son," Birlerion said as he led Jerrol over to the Kirshan leaders. He ignored Jerrol's startled glance and introduced Rivella and Yer'ota.

Jerrol held out his hand. "Medera, Sodera, I look forward to a long and happy partnership. I am glad you have already got to know Oscar."

Rivella smiled. "We are liaising closely. The Terolian guards will flourish, and you have chosen the perfect commander."

Maraine, who was standing beside them, laughed. "Captain, you have a Sentinal to wake. We will talk later. Join us for dinner before you return to Vespiri."

Jerrol hugged her and shook Viktor's hand. "It would be a pleasure. Birlerion, lead on."

They walked down the Tesene main street, garnering many curious glances. Jerrol and Niallerion in their archaic Lady's uniforms and Birlerion in his shimmering robes stood out as strangers. Even with the Medera camped outside their town, the people were suspicious.

"I don't think he will wake well," Birlerion said, breaking the silence.

"Why not?" Jerrol asked.

"He had a Darian."

"Oh! You managed alright."

"I had a purpose. The Lady told me to protect you. I could concentrate on that instead of Kaf'enir. I repressed her loss, along with a lot of other memories. It wasn't until I returned here to Terolia and was surrounded by the Family and Darians that I could no longer ignore it."

Jerrol squinted at him. "I am sorry. I had no idea. I don't know how you did it; I'm not sure I could. In fact, when I think of all that you have lost, I don't know how any of you do it. Remargaren is very different now."

"Not as different as you would think. There are still good people, and some remind you of the friends you had. Though you don't stop looking, as though expecting them to be around the corner."

"That's what I mean. How do you cope with that?"

"I don't know. But Kino makes it much better."

Jerrol grinned. "Trust you to make retrieving him so difficult."

"It wasn't my fault," Birlerion protested, and then he laughed as he realised Jerrol was teasing him.

They halted under the tall sentinal tree. "The last one," Jerrol said, staring at the slender silver trunk and the pointy emerald-green leaves. "I stopped in Marchwood on the way here, and only Elliarille and Ellaerion are left there. This is the last tree. You know, I thought the Lady would give me more seeds, that we would find more." He paused. "Tell me about Edrilion."

Birlerion sighed. "He was at the academy with Tagerill, Serill, and me. He was one of the first cadets from Terolia, along with Adil. We were in the same barracks. He helped me train Kaf'enir. It was Edril who suggested that Kaf'enir had Darian blood.

"He was posted to Melila when I was posted to East Mayer, which is now called East Watch. Part of my responsibility was to patrol the borders, along with Lorill. It wasn't long after the Lady formally created the watches that an Ascendant tried to enspell the Watch. We were sent to find out where he had been and who else had been affected.

"Lorill went north with Frener, and I went south with Adil. Eventually, we came across Edril in Melila, but the Ascendants had enspelled him. He was on his own with no one to back him up. After that, the Lady paired us up; we were always posted in pairs."

"Which explains why most Watches had two Sentinals," Jerrol murmured.

"Yes. Marguerite managed to release him, but Edril thought he had killed his Darian, so he tried to take his own life, unable to face living with the guilt. Marguerite didn't let him, but he was vulnerable. The last time I saw him, he was with Janis and Arkan at the Atolean camp. They promised to look after him. He needed the support of a Family around him, but how he got here, I don't know."

"Well, let's wake him and find out." Jerrol placed his hand on the tree and called Edrilion.

The air shimmered, and a tall, broad-shouldered Terolian stepped out. He had the typical blue-black curly hair and deep brown skin of the Terolians. Soft silver-green robes draped his stocky frame, and a wickedly curved scimitar hung at his waist. A glossy black stallion followed him, and Birlerion took a step back as he gasped in shock.

A broad smile spread over Edrilion's face. "Birlerion, what are you doing here?"

Birlerion stood stunned, his chest tight, his face paling.

"You have Der'inder with you." And then he clapped a hand over his mouth. "I—I'm sorry."

"Of course I do. Birlerion, I learnt my lesson. I promised you I would never leave him behind. I keep my promises." Edrilion stiffened as Birlerion continued to gape at him.

Jerrol stepped forward. "Edrilion, welcome home, and Der'inder, too. I am very glad to see you both."

Edrilion's brow creased, and his chin squared as he gazed at Birlerion. "Captain?" Edrilion asked, hesitating as he broke his gaze with Birlerion and looked around him. "Where are we? What happened?"

"You are in Tesene." Jerrol took a deep breath; it never got any easier. In a way, he was glad that this would be the last time he had to say this. "I am sorry, Edrilion, but I have to tell you that you've been asleep for over three thousand years. A lot has changed since you last walked this land."

Edrilion froze. "What?" He grabbed Birlerion and shook him. "What is he talking about? Where's Guerlaire?"

"He chose to leave with the Lady. Jerrol is the new Lady's Captain."

"He did what?" Edrilion asked as he struggled to accept what Birlerion had said. "Where's Kaf'enir?"

"She's not here," Birlerion said, his throat constricting as searing loss swept through him.

A dirty grey stallion came galloping down the main street, and a dust cloud rose around them as he skidded to a halt beside Birlerion. He nudged Birlerion. *"I'm here. You are not alone. You'll never be alone."*

Birlerion buried his face in Kin'arol's neck and shuddered.

"Birlerion? Where's Kaf'enir? What's going on?"

Jerrol ran his fingers through his hair, watching Birlerion with concern; this was not going as he had expected, but then, it never had. "Edrilion, there is a lot to explain.

Birlerion lost Kaf'enir. He has only just bonded with Kino here, and it is all still rather raw for him. Maybe if you come with us to the Atolean camp, we can explain."

Der'inder nudged forward, his midnight black hide gleaming in the sunlight. *"Birlerion? Is it true?"*

Kin'arol answered for him. *"Yes. Kaf'enir lived out her life three thousand years ago. She is no longer here. She was my many-times great-dam. I am a descendant of hers."*

"And mine?" Der'inder asked.

Birlerion stiffened.

Kin'arol's voice was soft. *"No, I'm sorry, Der'inder. Kaf'eder was your foal. He was not my sire."*

Edrilion gripped Der'inder's mane, his silver eyes wild. "I didn't do it again, did I? I swear I held the Lady close."

Birlerion wiped the tears off his cheeks. "You did great, Edril. The Lady protected you. I'm sorry. I didn't expect Der'inder to be with you, though I can't tell you how glad I am to see you both." He embraced Edrilion as he tried to control the grief roiling though him. "We lost so many."

"What? How? Who?"

Jerrol intervened. "Let's return to the camp. It will be easier to explain. Kayerille and Roberion are there," he said.

Edrilion brightened. "They are?" He embraced Birlerion in return. "I'm so glad to see you." He dropped his voice to a whisper. "I am so sorry. I didn't mean to upset you."

Birlerion gripped his arms. "You weren't to know. I just can't talk about her yet."

"I understand. I know how you feel. But who is this fine fellow with the horrible coat?" Edrilion asked, trying to ease the moment.

Birlerion chuckled. "This is Kino. Someone tried to steal him. Long story short, they dyed his coat to try to disguise him."

"My name is Kin'arol," the stallion murmured, and

Birlerion relaxed into his warm voice as his reassurance permeated his mind.

"Which obviously didn't work. I can't wait to hear the story." Edrilion looked at the elegant lines of the stallion, so at odds with the coat he wore. The Darian's head was as close to Birlerion's as he could get. *"Kin'arol, pleased to meet you. This is Der'inder."* Edrilion stroked the glossy neck of his Darian and looked at Jerrol. "Where is your Darian, Captain?"

Jerrol laughed. "I left her in Stoneford with my wife. Niallerion and I used the waystone."

"Niallerion, it's good to see you. I don't remember a waystone at Tesene," Edrilion said as they walked down the street back to the Atolean and Kirshan encampment, followed by the two Darians. The villagers peered at them, at the horses, and whispered to each other. "In fact, I don't remember Guerlaire ever coming this far south." He cast a nervous glance over his shoulder at the red mountain range on the horizon.

"Edrilion, much has happened since you've slept and we've awoken," said Birlerion, "but the Ascendants are no more. You don't have to worry about them ever again."

Huffing his breath out, Edrilion's shoulders dropped. "Thank the Lady. I'm not dreaming, am I? How long have you been … awake, Birlerion? What have I missed?"

"Everything!" Birlerion said with a wry grin. "Too much to explain now." He looked at Jerrol. "You know, I can't believe I've only been awake a year. So much has happened. I haven't stopped. No wonder I'm exhausted."

"You and me both," Jerrol said with a grin. He gripped Birlerion's arm. "You have time to rest now, so make the most of it. Return when you are ready. I understand how you feel. I feel much the same, and yet I can't understand the full extent of what you've been through. Edrilion has brought home just how much we have achieved in the last year, and I couldn't have done it without you."

Jerrol released Birlerion as they entered the camp, followed by a bemused Edrilion. Kayerille and Roberion mobbed Edrilion, and he was overwhelmed by his welcome.

After Edrilion had made his bow to the Mederas and Der'inder had been cosseted by all, and was now happily ensconced in the picket line with Kin'arol, munching on bali-weed, Edrilion reported to Jerrol as much as he could remember of those final days; evacuating the people from Melila, watching the fire mountains erupt, the boiling cauldron of the sea. His description of the acrid stench in the air and plumes of ash and grit that masked the sky and suffocated life had his audience gasping in horror.

As darkness descended, more introductions were made as the Families gathered and stories were swapped. The night came to an end, and Jerrol and Niallerion eventually returned to Old Vespers. The Sentinals sat around the fire, their quiet conversation lapsing for a moment when Edrilion suddenly sat up. His eyes went distant. "Who is Rigs?" he asked.

Birlerion chuckled. "Rigs is an Eleve. I think you'll find Der'inder may be in great demand. His bloodline will make you very rich."

Edrilion blew his cheeks out as he listened to Rigs and Der'inder converse. "It's truly been three thousand years?" he whispered.

"It has," Birlerion replied, equally softly.

"And Leyandrii is really gone?"

"Yes, though Marguerite is still with us, so don't go getting any ideas."

Edrilion blanched, and Birlerion laughed as he clapped him on the shoulder.

The next day, exhausted by all the explanations, Birlerion sat beside Yer'ota and stared out across the golden desert. "I think, my friend, it is time for us to go home. Kino and I will meet Roberion in Selir and continue from there. Oscar and Kayerille will head back to Mistra. Versillion is in Val'eria's safe hands. Edrilion and Der'inder have agreed to relocate to Fuertes with Rigs. We are not needed here any longer."

He gazed into the distance as he remembered Edrilion's eagerness to move away from the shadow of the red mountains. He would be happier with the Solari, and Rigs had already adopted Der'inder, watching him with that glow in her eyes.

"You will always be welcome," Yer'ota said. "Anytime."

Birlerion slapped his friend's shoulder. "I know. Thank you. But I want to go home."

"Then you should go."

A Week Later

Oscar tugged Kayerille back against his chest and rested his chin on her shoulder. He inhaled the spicy scent of her skin and nuzzled her neck. They stared out across the rolling dunes, gleaming gold and amber in the late afternoon sun. The sky was a clear cerulean blue that faded to yellow as it shimmered into the horizon.

"Do you miss him?" Oscar asked.

"Of course. Birlerion is family."

"I thought, to begin with, that you were closer."

"We looked out for each other. That's all."

"Even now? After all this time?"

Kayerille turned around in his embrace, cupped his face in her warm hands, and kissed him. Her face softened. "He was not meant for me. I am of Terolia. He is of Remargaren."

Oscar frowned. "What do you mean?"

"Haven't you noticed? No matter where Birlerion goes, he is accepted as family. Greens, Vespers, Stoneford, the Atolea, even Retarfu. I bet if he went to Birtoli, he'd find a way to make a home somewhere."

"I know home and family are important to him. Though Viktor said once that, even though he tries to make a family wherever he goes, he is still alone. He hasn't found it yet."

She leaned against him, smoothing her hand over his chest. "I think it's because he never had a home as a child. He'll never give up searching for one, but it's more than that. He is connected somehow, tightly bound to the fate of Remargaren, and he'll never forsake one part for another."

Oscar kissed her and tightened his embrace before staring at the distant dunes. "Do you think he'll ever find his home?"

"I hope so. Out of all of us, he deserves it the most."

"But not yet? It's not over, is it?"

"No. Somehow, I think the Lady still has work for us to do."

"Then we'll do it together," he said as he wrapped his arm around her waist, and they walked back into the slumbering city of Mistra.

THE END

Did you enjoy *Sentinals Recovery*? Then please leave a review. Reviews help authors raise awareness of their books and drive visibility to other readers. A bit like book matchmaking!

. . .

Amazon direct review links:

UK:　　　　　　　　Amazon.co.uk/review/create-review?
&asin=B09HN6J7W5

USA:　　　　　　　Amazon.com/review/create-review?&
asin=B09HN6J7W5

CANADA:　　　　　　Amazon.ca/review/create-review?&
asin=B09HN6J7W5

You can find out more about my books, sign up to my newsletter and receive a free ebook of *Sentinals Stirring* at www.helengarraway.com.

ACKNOWLEDGMENTS

This novella wasn't originally in my plan, (which is why it is book 3.5!) but I just couldn't fit Birlerion bonding with his Darian into *Sentinals Justice*. He never had the opportunity to return to Greenswatch and I thought it was too important an event not to write, and then as it evolved it became even more relevant to the whole series, and I couldn't resist the opportunity to explore Versillion and Oscar a little more. I hope you agree.

If it wasn't for my mother, Margaret, instilling in me a love of books, and reading, I would never be writing these words today. I wish I had started writing earlier so I could have shared this moment with her because I know she would have loved my characters and the world they inhabit.

I am thankful for my darling daughter, Jennifer, who encouraged me to take the step and self-publish, and go social, and build a website, and take to twitter.

The wonderful designers at Miblart designed my beautiful cover, and Tom from FictiveDesigns (https:// www.fictive-designs.com/maps) drew the exquisite maps of Vespiri and Terolia.

I hope you enjoy reading *Sentinals Recovery* as much as I

enjoyed writing it, and I look forward to continuing the adventure with you in my fourth full length novel, *Sentinals Across Time*, which will arrive in 2022.

Other books in the Sentinal Series:

Book 0.5: Sentinals Stirring (Novella)
Book 1: Sentinals Awaken
Book 2: Sentinals Rising
Book 3: Sentinals Justice
Book 3.5: Sentinals Recovery (Novella)
Book 4: Sentinals Across Time (to be published)

ABOUT THE AUTHOR

Helen Garraway lives in the UK and has been writing about the world of Remargaren, a fantasy world of her creation since 2016.

Sentinals Awaken, which was Helen's debut fantasy novel, won the 2021 Readers' Favorite Finalist Award in the Epic Fantasy category. It was followed by Sentinals Rising which was released on March 17th 2021 and Sentinals Justice, which was published on 7th September 2021.

An avid reader of many different fiction genres, a love she inherited from her mother, Helen writes fantasy novels and enjoys paper crafting and scrapbooking as an escape from the pressure of working for a Video conferencing company, as a Product Manager.

Having graduated from the University of Southampton with a Degree in Politics and International Relations, she remains an active member of their alumni.

Lightning Source UK Ltd.
Milton Keynes UK
UKHW020635241021
392748UK00002B/3